I0646763

THE LADY IN THE LOFT
CATACLYSMS IN THE COSMOS

Robert C. Jones

A publication of

Eber & Wein Publishing

Pennsylvania

The Lady in the Loft
Cataclysms in the Cosmos

Copyright © 2025 by Robert C. Jones

All rights reserved under the International and Pan-American copyright
conventions. No part of this book may be reproduced, stored in a retrieval system, or
transmitted in any form, electronic, mechanical, or by other means, without written
permission of the author.

Library of Congress
Cataloging in Publication Data

ISBN 978-1-60880-808-3

Proudly manufactured in the United States of America by

Eber & Wein Publishing
Pennsylvania

Dedicated to our three grandsons—Brandon, Joshua, Justin—who always enjoy a good story fictionalized or otherwise and to the Romeo District Library and Kezar branches of the Romeo District Library system.

To Nonna—a lifelong companion, wife, mother, and mother-in-law—for keeping our family (*familia*) together in the real world of love and kindness and for her soulful presence for all to feel her joy.

Tribute to Janina Parrott Jacobs for Janina's character in "Lady in the Loft."

Tribute to Al Beauleaux for putting me on the right path for the lessons Henry David Thoreau taught us all about life and living.

CONTENTS

PROLOGUE

Gaia, the Greek goddess for Mother Earth, was changing her mood from nurturing, caring, and looking after her brood (children) to anger, hostility, and a need to wreak havoc on all inhabitants (earthlings) who lived on land or sea and who were in past times eternally dependent on her vibrant warmth and consistent good nature for their survival.

This change over time brought ravaging fires, destructive earthquakes, tornadoes, and hurricanes, which affected all earthly creatures. Populations around this globe were stricken, and some perished due to a lack of food and water.

Whole existences of certain animals and plants died out. They were never again a part of the natural order of this earth, which was always ordered thusly: life, domain, kingdom, phylum, class, order, family, genus, species.

Long ago in ancient times, Gaia and Uranus bore twelve children, the Titans: Oceanus, Hyperion, Coeus, Crius, Iapetus, Cronus, Mnemosyne, Themis, Phoebe, Theia, Tethys, and Rhea.

The Titans ruled from Mt. Orthys. For a long time—as time then was measured—they used their powers to keep the peace and to allow those under their rule in their universe and on Earth to go about their lives, not to disturb the "natural order of these organisms."

But now Gaia was enraged. Her mate Uranus, and father to the Titans, betrayed her by hiding their children's bodies where she could not find them.

Gaia then asked all her children, "Which of you will help me form a plan to punish Uranus and bring him to justice?"

Only Cronus responded to Gaia's cry for help with these words:

"Mother, I am willing to undertake and carry through your plan, whatever that may be. I have no respect for our infamous father, since he was the one who started using violence."

Cronus was the most powerful male god, and he alone punished his father. This violent upheaval within the Titan family caused widespread destruction on Mother Earth below.

Storms on the oceans caused all sea creatures to tremble; some perished and were never seen again. On land, fires raged in the primal forests, and many of these land creatures also succumbed to the brutality of the wild weather.

The human population was also affected by the domestic disturbances of the Titan families. After Uranus was defeated and punished, the twelve Titans and Gaia tried to bring peace and tranquility to their universe, both in the sky and on Earth. But there was much arguing and jealousy among the siblings and with Gaia.

Each of the twelve Titans ruled over a specific part of their world and the world below. As many eons of time passed into ancient history, each ruler lost control over their appointed role and fell into disfavor with Gaia, their Mother Protector.

Oceanus, Titan of the great river, who possessed a peaceful nature, let this river overflow its banks, leading to floods and lost lives.

Hyperion, the Titan of the sun and light and father of Helios, let the shadows cover over the sun, and darkness prevailed in the sky and on Earth. This chilled the earth, and the celestial seasons were far out of rhythm.

Coeus, the Titan associated with intellect and prophecy, cast his dull nature on his fellow gods and all creatures below. The progress of human enterprise regressed. Mankind stopped its thinking process. This dullness of enterprise and character became the norm.

Crius, who ruled the southern part of the world, relinquished his position and became lazy and slothful.

Lopetus, father to Prometheus, Epimetheus, and Menoetius, gave up his paternal nature.

Mnemosyne, goddess of memory and mother of the muses, could not reflect on the past, nor make intelligent decisions with everyday living conditions, nor project, with any foresight, what the future may be all about.

She also did not encourage the gods or earthlings to dream of becoming poets, painters, or writers. She let the dullness of everyday life prevail, providing no hope for any creature to strive to become a better god or human being.

Themus was the god of justice, wisdom, and good counsel. In the sky and on earth, laws were broken. Those responsible were not brought to justice. Judges and judicial counselors provided no insight into how these laws should be adjudicated.

The gods and humans suffered irreparable damage from those vandals, scoundrels, and thieves whose lawlessness preyed on these aggrieved souls.

Phoebe, goddess of wisdom and prophecy, likewise was derelict in her duty.

Theia and Tethys also neglected their roles and fell into disrepute.

Thus, over many revolutions and seasons, the earth spun out of control, the inhabitants hovelling, hiding in darkened spaces.

The land and sea were no longer viable places of growth and renewal. The inhabitants ceased to work on finding sustenance to feed their bodies and souls. Plagues became the norm. Masses of the living died, becoming fodder, and just became dust in the course of all these human events.

An unsettling nature existed among the gods; those who were from different clans, societies, and dynasties displayed their anger and wrath in a variety of temperaments and displays of angst and rebellion.

Of all the Titans, only Rhea, daughter of Gaia and Uranus, came forth to pose a solution to these unsettling events. She was the Titan goddess of motherhood and fertility. She married Cronus, her brother, and bore the eight basic Olympian gods. Thus, a new regime of Greek gods appeared.

However, a savage war broke out between the two factions, the Titans and the Olympians.

This war, the Titanomachy, lasted ten years. It was led by Zeus, the great leader of the Olympians. The earth below was scorched. The land was barren, producing little or no food crops.

The seasonal cycles were out of rhythm. The tropics produced arctic-like temperatures. The colder regions of Earth produced sweltering hot weather.

Fires continued to blaze across the landscapes of the world.

Now earthquakes have begun to emerge from below the surface, destroying whole towns. The seas were drying up. The homes of many sea creatures were lost. The hope of survival for the remaining humans on Earth was slim. The end of the war couldn't come soon enough.

Zeus and his army fought hard over those ten years to defeat the Titans. Finally, the war ended. It was time for the Olympians to take power. They would rule from Mt. Olympus. Each Olympian took his position and firmly established his power over the Universe Cosmos and those creatures below.

The Titans were imprisoned in the land of Tartarus, where they were rendered helpless and powerless, yet still had some influence in shaping events and the future of the cosmos.

Zeus was the great leader representing the sky and lightning. His will was powerful. Poseidon was the god of the sea and expressed a wide range of emotions, with an instinctual nature. His enemy was Odysseus.

Hades was the god of the underworld. He took souls into the depths of the psyche and into the unconscious.

Apollo was the god of the sun, warmth, nourishment, and security. Hermes was the messenger god who communicated with other gods regarding the various affairs of the Olympians and the civilizations below. Ares was the god of war. It was his job now to keep the peace by keeping his enemies under control. Hephaestus was god of the forge. He was a craftsman, creating many architectural splendors. His wife was Aphrodite. Dionysus was the god of ecstasy and wine. He was a mystic wanderer traveling throughout the cosmos. He was also an ecstatic lover. His wife was Ariadne.

All the Olympian gods were now in place. For a period, perhaps eons, the order of rhythm and the seasons conflicted among the gods; both the Olympians and others were kept in check.

Over time, these gods began to clash among themselves. There were plagues, wars—the Trojan War in particular, the Wrath of Poseidon, the jealousies of Hera, and the bitter fighting between Poseidon and Athena, which caused the universe to tremble and the world below to once again begin to disintegrate with fires, floods, and plagues—worldwide destruction.

Gaia bore creatures (Gigantes) that opposed the Olympians, especially Zeus, for he banished the Titans to the underworld. Gigantomacy was the term for the war fought against the Olympians by these giant creatures.

Again, it was Rhea who came forward to propose a plan to restore peace among the gods. She was angry at Zeus for his many transgressions. He used his warlike powers again and again to strike his enemies down and even to keep his fellow Olympians under his control. He spread his gossip and foul comments.

Rhea knew she alone would not be able to approach Gaia and ask her, even beg her, to stop her own warlike crusade against the Olympians—especially Zeus. As the story goes, Rhea gave Cronus (her mate) a stone wrapped in swaddling clothes instead of her newborn Zeus. He was then raised on the island of Crete.

Zeus forced Cronus to disgorge his siblings, the Titans. Rhea then owed Zeus many favors over time (eons), which she bestowed on Zeus. But now, because of Zeus' numerous affairs and nefarious activities, Rhea broke away from him. She knew the gods were disrupting, even destroying, their own cosmos, let alone upsetting the seasonal rhythms, the land and sea below.

There must be some human entity among the billions of earthlings below who could persuade Gaia of her wayward ways and could help to reconcile the myriad differences among the many gods in the cosmos—mainly the Olympians and even the Titans who still had some small measure of power.

After all, the Olympians, despite their many arguments and clashes, still, with much wise counsel, could be reigned in and once again bring peace over the next millennium to each other and to the earthlings below.

Rhea was, to be sure, the Titan goddess of motherhood and fertility, and was the mother of the Olympians. She and Gaia had much in common; both were nurturing, and they spread the warmth and beauty of their maternal nature throughout the ages, allowing all gods/goddesses and earthlings to grow and prosper from their eternal outpouring of affection and life-affirming messages. Rhea was to seek one of these earthly creatures who possessed these qualities, especially the trait of love in its many forms.

When first coming to power, the Olympians expressed in their ideal form these qualities:

>1. Eros—passionate, romantic love; a powerful and intense emotion.
>2. Phillia—love of friendship, characterized by affection, intimacy, and shared experiences.
>3. Storge—love that exists among family members; natural affection and care.
>4. Agape—selfless, unconditional, and universal form of love.

5. Pragma—practical, enduring love based on reason and shared goals; long-term relationships.

6. Philautia—self-love; seen as a positive trait; may sometimes be self-centeredness.

7. Xenia—a type of love displaying hospitality toward foreigners and travelers.

1

The weather report for this evening predicted another violent storm for the region. This time, hail and damaging winds would cause significant destruction, knocking down trees and power lines. No power for the residents of the county. But then what else was new?

Over the past five years, it seemed the seasons had lost their natural form. Most folks would say, "Mother Nature is just playing some awful tricks on us."

But in this rural area, these people were dependent on their small plots of land for survival. Rarely over that period of time did most farmers bring all their production to fruition. According to the best farm bureau reports, only about twenty-five percent of the crops after planting were harvested.

For this one-centennial homestead, the ruinous nature of business led this family to begin the process of selling the farm.

"Another bad storm a comin'. Batten down the hatches." Gramps kept his pipe lit as the storm moved in. Lightning flashed from the sky, making the night air appear as bright as day.

The family scurried to the storm cellar. A candle was lit. Along with Gramps, his wife, Bessie, his mother, Mary, her husband, Howard, their daughter, Lisa, and their son, Bobby, they now huddled in a sort of cowering posture. Nothing new. Area residents, the whole region, the whole state—frankly, the nation and the world—on eternal alert.

These days of reckoning added up to half a decade, a world order run amok. A power line sounded its alarm. Close to the house was a buzzing noise. A tree toppled against the house.

They heard more sounds, one sounding like a freight train then a *whooshing* sound, loud and blasting. The barn door exploded off its hinges. It went sailing to parts unknown. Windows on the house were smashed.

Would the storm cellar hold? The air held an electric sensation, crackling with energy. A foul-smelling gas erupted. The residents of this bunker, weakened by sickness, began to decline.

Their dog whimpered, tearing up. Just as this part of the storm passed, hail the size of softballs pummeled the dwelling. The siding was shredded. The columns on the front porch collapsed. No more Ionic limbs to hold up the small roof.

"Hear that?" Gramps first to speak.

"Hear what?" Bessie broke in.

"Precisely. The storm has passed." Gramps got up, and the others moved restlessly to their feet. Howard bumped his head on the low ceiling. He lost his usual calm demeanor. "To heck with this place. This way to survive. Can't stand it. No way to make a living. Sure as all get out, we can't go on like this. Now to clean up another mess. Most of our farming neighbors are in the same boat. Even the big-time farmers are going bankrupt. Worldwide droughts, lakes dryin' up, fires destroying crops . . . Armageddon I tell ya."

Bessie spoke up: "Let's get out of this bunker mentality. Howard, you were always the grumpy one in the family. When we get our place cleaned up, we'll do a pow-wow . . . take stock of what we have left here and where we're goin'. Our place is paid for. Lock, stock, and barrel. No need to panic. We're a loving, caring family."

"Well, ain't that just the cat's meow?" Gramps climbed out of the bunker into the open air. "Kept the pipe lit during the storm; now that the storm's passed, dang thing went out."

The evening air still smelled of burnt wires and the smell of burning rubber. The horses in the barn kicked up a storm of their own, still very agitated.

Felix, their outdoor cat, jumped from the kitchen windowsill, a window not blown out by the storm, onto a board part of the barn door and incurred a splinter in her paw.

A local company was hired to clean up the debris. The barn door needed to be replaced. The siding would be replaced by another company in a week or so. Damage to other farms in the region was far more extensive, resulting in a loss of livestock that had been left to fend for themselves.

A farm bureau meeting in a week or so would initiate the process to request federal assistance; perhaps the state would provide local support with some farm aid.

Bobby went to his room right after the storm. He was growing into his teenage years and feeling changes inside himself, which were puzzling, mystifying, and almost morbid, although he didn't know the meaning of that word. The term *rage* would be better suited to his current temperament. Perhaps a bit of confusion thrown in for good measure. His self-directed dialogue verged on self-loathing, and that term, too, was too difficult for him to comprehend.

He thought he was doing everything in his power to "make things right" for the family: giving some of his paper route money to the family's general fund, getting a reasonable price for eggs. He was friends with a fellow student whose parents raised chickens. Mission accomplished.

He tried to convince his mom to get into the chicken business as a family venture. Too much money and too much inventory to acquire, his mother kept telling him.

He worked hard around the place. Cleaned out the barns. Worked on the tractor. Plowed up the acreage in the spring, with dad's assistance, of course. And this past summer, the inside of the home had to be painted, and he helped there, too. Now the headaches were coming, fast and furious. He couldn't tell Mom or Dad, and certainly not Grandma and Gramps. And leave his sister out of it. Anything he told her would not be kept secret for long. He thought the term was *tattletale*. She seemed to get a kick out of telling Mom and Dad anything she could find out about him. It seemed that any situation that happened in school could get him into trouble.

Her own twelve-year-old mind and body was beginning to change, *morph*, as Bobby thought, into a strange, unimaginable creature, gory and ugly to the core, with a torso growing out of proportion to the arms and legs and a head growing to the size of the largest watermelon in the patch that could spin around to 360 degrees with eyes in the back and side. And talk, talk, talk. Where was the place—the button to push or the cord to pull to shut off the machine that he knew was somewhere deep in her throat?

So, he found sanctuary here in his room, the smallest bedroom in the house, built over the garage, the ceiling coming to a peak, not very high up.

He hung his World War II planes on wires. The big B-29 Bomber hung down within a few feet of the pillow on the bed where he rested his head for a supposed good night's sleep. These days, however, that was a rare occurrence. And the headaches continued, often without warning. They lasted a day or so, then went away, only to return in a few days, getting continuously worse. His reading habits varied. A large bookcase was placed against a wall just a few feet from the end of the bed.

He liked detective stories. An odd hero of his was Freddie the Pig, a series of stories about a pig detective who solved puzzling mysteries on a farm.

But then the usual Hardy Boys series kept him busy reading, as did the Nancy Drew mysteries. Recently, upon reaching his first teenage year, his interest turned to the gods and goddesses of the cosmos, a new concept he had learned about and continually wondered about.

What was the difference between the words *universe* and *cosmos*? Both terms contained the word 'organized' in them.

A universe was a distinct field of province, or thought, or reality that forms a closed system of self-inclusive and independent organization. The term cosmos had a similar meaning in the dictionary. His Merriam-Webster was always within reach.

So, who were these gods and goddesses, and how real were they? At least to the people who lived in the past – even before recorded time?

For Bobby, this was an escape. He knew the terms *reality* and *fantasy*. His family problems—disputes with his sister, and not knowing what the future would be like—all dissolved when he was thinking of these gods and goddesses.

Some, he knew, were heroes and could help people, maybe all of mankind. Another term he came to know and understand was the word *myth*.

A myth, he knew, was a way for people in a country to explain their way of life; their traditions; the way they treated each other; and who their friends and enemies were. These myths have been passed down from generation to generation. There were truths to these myths, though, for the most part, they were made-up stories.

Before the advent of Christianity, people believed in these gods. Each one had his/her personality, but they all affected those humans below in either positive or negative ways.

Bobby sat alone in his room, ear tuned to the vent where he heard his parents and grandparents discussing his, they proclaimed, rich fantasy life.

"Time to get that boy some help. Get him to a . . . what's the term—head shrinker. The boy's out of control. Not natural cooped up in his room readin' them stories 'bout fantasy characters," Gramps said, going on, his pipe shooting out large puffs of smoke.

Bessie broke in: "Oh, let the boy be. Just growin' pains. Body growin', mind growin'. I've seen him grow from a colicky baby to this stage in his life. He'll find himself someday. Give him time to grow into adulthood," she said, her voice trailing off as she got up and went to the kitchen—her place of refuge during stressful moments.

"He's listened to my stories, our family's history—all real life. He might say they're myths. Not necessarily true. Time Uncle Charley's tool and die shop up on a riverbank. Bad storm.

Rain. Flooding. The whole building slid into the Big Hearted River. He regrouped. Moved to the city. Started over. Success.

"Or our family's famous athlete, cousin Ralph. Beat that Olympic runner in an exhibition race at the Big House. It was quite a night of celebration for our family.

"No myth there. And how about our Mary, a real athlete. Started that basketball program at the college. Came to be the varsity team. Still there." Gramps' voice now trailed off.

Bobby hunkered down under his covers. He told himself that all these bad events around the world, his own farmland—crops dying out, bad soil—could not make payroll; his dad would say time and time again, was the result of the angry gods looking down over the entirety of the earth's surface, casting spells on the inhabitants.

Gaia (Mother Earth) was, for some reason, angry, casting floods, fires, and climate changes upon the human and animal populations.

Bobby drifted off to sleep, thinking about myths, stories, traditions, gods, and goddesses.

2

The old Gothic church, with its cherubs and gargoyles, conveyed joy and also a menacing message to the congregants who entered the portals, hoping to achieve, or at least meet, some form of salvation upon exiting these same portals.

How much of this individual endeavor was human effort, and how much came from some form of divine intervention? One could only surmise from his/her faith-based position.

The congregation would chant their praises in biblical form, hoping to catch the spirit of whoever or whatever would respond in kind, sending some message to the faithful that these prayers would be answered positively, which would constitute the beginnings or continuation of some form of healing process.

The family attended weekly mass, Grandpa and Grandma sitting on the aisle, enabled by canes, often seen poking one another as they made their way to their places. They remained seated, preferring not to strain their bodies during the service.

"If I kneel, I'll never be able to get up. The whole body hurts nowadays. Gettin' old is not for sissies." Gramps was known to make this proclamation again and again.

The rest of the family slid in down the row in the same seats each week—always the fourth aisle back.

Other older congregants, whose hearing was impaired or who had given more funds to the church than was usually requested, sat further up in rows one, two, or three.

Gramps again would comment, "Those folks are higher up in the religion, money-giving food chain." He would then chuckle. "But then money buys most things—just have to have enough of those greenbacks."

Bobby sat beside his mom in his white, starched, collared shirt, blue pants, shined Buster Brown shoes, and a belt tight around his middle. The change of seasons would produce a variety of coats—a winter heavy wool parka, a spring lighter-weight coat, a summer very light-weight or no coat, and a fall coat varying with the change of the season.

Mom would instruct him, "Now, before the mass, make sure your bladder is emptied. I know you're a regular fellow with your number two."

Dad would add his advice, "You know how to sit up straight. You know the routine. Stick with the script, young man."

Bobby heard those requests week after week and found them tiresome. *Same old, same old*, he told himself.

If there was to be any further interest in this worshipping process, he thought he must find some other interest within the confines of this building to sustain his interest.

This morning, Bobby focused his sights on the stained-glass windows above. Light penetrated through the mosaics of the family—Joseph, Mary, and Jesus. Other windows portrayed the biblical story with the wise men and the manger scene—one in which God is seen blowing his breath of air through the clouds, lighting up the sky. This morning in church, these scenes excited his conscious being. Never before in the church had he experienced such emotion.

For years, he had been attending services and had made little note of the singer in the loft who also handled duties on the massive pipe organ.

At some services, a choir was present, typically consisting of six males and six females. During the holiday season, they were dressed in fancy robes, and their voices seemed to ascend to the apex of the church ceiling.

His mother would tell him that these heavenly sounds would stir the angels above to peer at the congregation and would assist in lifting everyone's spirit with each note, coaxing those angels to penetrate the souls of those who were ready to accept salvation.

"Blessed be God forever."

Bobby was drawn today to the lady in the loft who made those sounds on the organ along with a choir, even though most of the time she sang without a choir's assistance.

I should introduce myself, he thought, *and ask her for a tour of that space, the choir loft, up high in the back of the church. I'll tell Mom I'm going to walk home since it's a nice spring day. Say hi to some neighbors. Be pleasant. Clear my mind. That frightening storm was gone, right?*

Permission granted. *Just spend a few minutes. Don't dawdle when walking home. Be home in time for Sunday dinner. Don't stop at the Emporium*—candy heaven for the kids in the neighborhood.

The stairs were steep and narrow, the climb steeper than he anticipated. Out of breath when he reached the top, he found a padded chair. His frame plopped on the chair just as a large satchel was dropped on that same space.

This area, the balcony, was dark. The organ, situated in the middle, was a monster with pipes shooting upward in various lengths, like tendrils reaching toward the ceiling.

The occupant in the room, whose back was turned, came around, sensing a lifeform behind.

"Excuse me," she said. "I don't know my own strength. Just threw the bundle on the chair. Didn't see you there. Where'd you come from? Quiet one you are. Service over. Me, Janina, and you, young man, are—" her head jerked downward, eyes rolling.

She switched to another thought. "So the service, okay by you? Off-key this morning, and voice cracking. Picked some tricky hymns. Too many key changes.

"Weather's changin' again. Barometric pressure is stuffing up my head. Too much nasal quality in my singing voice now.

"You've got a big family here every week, right on time. No dawdling. You've been a congregant longer than I've been here. Is two years being a music director here considered being a semi-rookie?"

It was then Bob saw her come out of the shadow, fully facing him. He picked up the satchel, which was filled with books and papers, and placed it on the floor by a table covered with sheet music, vases filled with flowers, and an extensive dictionary.

"Bob's the name. Just wanted to say hi. Never been up here. This place—er loft—seems older, dustier than the rest of the church."

It was then that he thought himself rude to make such a comment. But the thought stuck. It was dark and dank, with cobwebs covering a stained-glass window, preventing much light from entering.

A chandelier hung from the ceiling directly over the organ, with several bulbs burnt out. Long strands of dust connected the

light fixture to the bottom of the stained-glass window, a high-wire act for any daring arachnid.

"Okay, your name's Bob. Mine's Janina. Glad to make your acquaintance. But I have to run—got a service, a funeral, to attend to," she said, her voice drifting off. She sidled by Bob, looked at him directly eye to eye, and stopped suddenly.

"Come back here Wednesday at 4:00 PM after choir practice. I'll show you our organ and how I work it. Say, we need more members in our choir. I'm sure your voice will blend in with the rest of the singers. You'd be a welcomed addition—the youngest member by far." She reached the top steps and turned to wait for a reply.

Looking puzzled, Bob stammered, "Sure, okay. After school. Your organ is mammoth. Bigger than I thought," he said, his face reddening as he realized how that might be interpreted.

Without hesitation, Janina smiled broadly, her dimples prominent. Her shoulder-length mane abruptly swished. "Oh, and when you come up here, don't mind the ghosts. They like the cobwebs and the dark shadows up here. And just let the angels have their way. There's only one, the Angel of Death, we're worried about. Too ta loo, Bob."

She clutched the satchel to her chest and bounded down the steps two at a time, leaving Bob to notice a large spider spinning a web on the chandelier, then waiting for an unsuspecting insect to get caught in her trap.

The altar, from where he was standing, seemed miles away. His place up front, as well as all the pews, were within close range.

This Janina lady had the best view. To think her voice carried throughout this vintage shrine was a testament—there was a biblical term he was familiar with—to her powerful voice and her ability to blend the organ music with the singing.

He had always just assumed the organ played itself. He took two steps back and faced what he told himself was the console. He would ask her to explain how this machine worked. What made the sounds high, low—the various pitches. And all these plugs to operate.

All this angel business and ghosts, he was sure was just her way of entertaining me. She seemed to be quite alive, active, smiling, talkative—quite the showperson, he surmised.

Okay, so 4:00 PM this coming Wednesday at the loft. Maybe I can tell Mom and Dad I'm volunteering on the grounds and maintenance committee. I'll at least talk to the head custodian and make myself known. Maybe even volunteer to clean up some of the grounds around the church.

There was a large garden behind the church. The pathway was constructed entirely of brickwork, paid for by the congregants in memory of a loved one. The path for the Stations of the Cross needs weeding all the time. He heard the head custodian say he did not want to spray the weeds with a poisonous defoliant, so perhaps he could do it by hand with a weed picker. Churchgoers won't be poisoned.

His parents did wonder a bit. "My boy is gettin' on the right track; his faith growing. I told you, Mom, all that talk about sitting up straight in church, mindin' his P's and Q's, staying quiet, listening to His word is payin' off." His father broke the silence in the parlor the evening before Bob would go again to the loft to discuss with Janina how the organ worked.

"I hope all his sullenness is just a phase. Good boy and all. Teen years, I guess, cause many changes in one's personality."

"Not breakin' out in those ugly pimples yet," Gramps chimed in. "Gotta have some fun with the kid."

"Leave him alone. How were you as a teenager back in the day, Reece? A lot of trouble, don't ya know," said Grandma, getting in the final word.

Bob and his sister were in separate bedrooms across the hall from each other. Bob lay outstretched on his back, arms behind his head, peering up at the war planes dangling from their wires, ready to do battle.

I wonder what it would be like to pilot one of those jets? And how high can they go? And how far above those planes is what is called outer space! And what is beyond that? Bob had many questions and few concrete answers. His headaches continued to bother him. *Sleep. See that lady in the loft tomorrow after school. And how does that lady get such a roaring good sound out of that big machine?*

3

The steps seemed even steeper this afternoon. *Why was this place so dark?* His thoughts were interrupted.

"Well, well, as I live and breathe . . . keeping a commitment. Good work!"

Bob stopped abruptly as this form scurried around picking up music books, straightening some music stands, and folding the satchel she had left clutching to her chest this past Sunday. "Well, now you can sit, but I've got business here to attend to. I'll be upright."

The choir was way too noisy today. Too many loud, overbearing voices. The old men especially seemed to want to bellow like wounded bulls. The ladies just wanted to squeak like wounded robins.

"Glad you're here. Your journey is just beginning. I'd like to introduce you to the hierarchy of the angels. No matter what position they find themselves in, they're aching, hurt beyond belief. Crying out. Their whole divine world is out of rhythm; no natural order anymore."

What did all this have to do with Bob's visit and how the organ worked? He was at a loss for words. He sat staring up at the grime and dirt on the stained-glass window.

"Now the first level. Those seraphims aren't zealous anymore. There's no spunk in 'em. Maybe they're lazy or have just given up, but there's no energy. The cherubim lack the knowledge they should have and can't make intelligent heavenly decisions. And the thrones lack judgment. They can't decide what's right and what's wrong.

"Then there are those dominions—second level. Not very humane these days. The Virtues aren't taking care of the elements and planets. Don't seem to care anymore either. The powers angels aren't fighting against evil.

"The lowest hierarchy—the principalities, the archangels, and the common lower level angels, including the messengers and guardians of we who dwell here on Earth—well, wings not flopping, moping, listless. No one here on Earth is receiving any of their blessings. Sad, I tell ya. Just plain criminal.

"Communities here on Earth are breaking down. No one trusts each other. We're all just disconnected visitors soaring around aimlessly on our big rock.

"There, I've said my peace—er—not so peaceful. Don't understand all this yakking, do ya? Sorry, Bob, you'll have to come back next Wednesday. Gotta run. Okay, I'll tell ya how this contraption works then."

Bob, still sitting, watched as she dashed by him, clutching that satchel to her chest.

"Oh, by the way, my name's Janina Jerusalem. Now that we have been formally introduced, please call me J.J. And one last note—when you come on Wednesday, be prepared to discuss the term *portal*. I would like you to explain both the literal meaning and the metaphorical—or deeper—meaning, especially as it relates to some form of mysticism. Not to get away from our faith, but just an extension of our trust in each other and our divine presence among the elements of truth in the cosmos."

Bob thought he saw a puff of smoke as she disappeared, leaping down the steps three at a time.

There now was a distinct chill in the air. He zipped up his jacket and looked around at the vast expanse of this church, noticing more than one side altar, candles glowing for those intentions. Keep the faith.

However, this music director has now given him an assignment. Learn the term *portal*. To what end, he thought?

And this talk of the cosmos. Elements of truth. And what is this divine presence?

He just wanted to know how this mammoth machine worked. He'd come next Wednesday, hopefully, to find out.

As he descended the stairs, he looked up at the stained-glass window and saw an owl peering at him through the dust-covered pane. It was more than just a stare. Its head revolved as the form on the stairs, one step at a time, made it to the bottom and out a side door.

He looked back at the structure as he walked a pathway home. Two dogs chained to a post began to growl and bark loudly as he passed them. With teeth exposed and foam dripping from their mouths, their beady eyes focused on Bob.

Running was not an option. Bob stayed calm and walked smartly, one foot ahead of the other. When almost home, he peered into the clear blue sky and noticed two large objects—birds, he thought. They were flying in circles, hovering overhead, flying within a hundred feet or so of the roof of his homestead.

His dreams that night were frightening. A confusing array of animals darted in and out of his mental state.

There were objects, animals on land running aimlessly across a dust-covered plain. A stag and a bear galloped side by side. A large horse followed, its stride catching up with the two animals ahead of it.

Now a peacock appeared, spreading its plumage, its colors bright and mesmerizing. Suddenly, the focus shifted to a large pond, where the sounds of swamp creatures pierced the night air. A swan appeared, elegant and regal in stature, but moving aimlessly around in circles.

The scene then shifted to a larger body of water. An ocean. A dolphin was seen swimming smoothly at first, then, knowing it was going off course, began squeaking, creating eerie sounds as it tried to reach out to its family, but was now lost in the vast expanse of the sea.

His headache reached a crescendo, the pain crushing his temples. Night sweats took over. Sleep came, but only for an hour or so. He awakened feeling weak, nauseous, with a dry mouth, and out of breath.

This condition lasted all week, right up to the following Wednesday, when he would again see Janina—J.J. Would he talk to her about these dreams? Probably not. He searched his dictionary for the meaning of the term *portal*. A doorway, a gate, or other entrance, especially a large, imposing one.

So why would J.J. want him to know this term? He was hoping he could just ask questions as to how the organ worked—there wasn't much else to discuss—then leave. Just attend Sunday masses as usual. Follow his parents' directions. Be proper. Mind one's manners. Be polite to fellow congregants. Stay out of trouble. But his senses told him otherwise.

Again, this midweek, the church appeared empty. Even the custodian could not be found making his rounds, cleaning, dusting, and tending to his business.

He did spot a person kneeling and praying at one of the side altars.

"Welcome, young man. Come up to my lair. Busy, don't you know. The choir is off its mark. Can't get this choir to stick to their parts. Sopranos want to be altos. Altos want to be tenors and so on. What can I do for you? Nasty weather, isn't it? Bad storm two days ago in New Delhi on the Ganges, don't you know?"

"I came," Bob started, catching a mouthful of air, "to just ask how the organ you play works—those big pipes up to the ceiling."

"You could have gone to the library and checked out a book on organs. But okay, you're here. Not much time today. I'll make it quick. Well, the air rushes through a pipe, which vibrates and produces a sound. Look at all these pipes here. Different shapes and lengths create different pitches and timbres.

"We use these devices called stops to produce those pitches and timbre. A typical stop might be an eight-foot pitch, meaning its longest pipe is eight feet long, producing a sound at the normal pitch for that stop. Other common pitches include sixteen feet, four feet, and two feet, each sounding an octave lower, or higher, respectively."

She began opening and closing stops, producing notes on the scale.

Turning to Bob, she said, "So enough of this subject. You know why you are *really* here, don't you? Give me the definition of a portal." She came closer and faced him, one foot ahead of the other, ready to sprint ahead, sail off over the balcony. She stopped abruptly and tripped over a wastebasket, hands coming down on a table."

"A portal is a doorway. A gate or other entrance, especially a large, imposing one." He thought that to be enough of an answer.

"Only the beginning, dear boy. Only the beginning. Other worlds out there. All the rhythms in the cosmos are out of sync.

"Enough talk for this meeting. I got something for you." She reached into a box and came out with a jacket. It was light-weight and zipped up the front, featuring two pockets and bright colors that appeared in streaks on the front and back. "We'll meet next week again. Wear this jacket when you come. More storms are on the way this week. Fires in Nepal. Amazon rainforest dry-in' up. Up is down. Down is up. Seeds not germinating. Gardens parched. It's going to be a bad growing season again. Your homestead is going under Bob. I see a sale on the horizon. Just get here on time next week. Gotta run." She loped down the steps and was gone. Maybe a side door.

Bob sat. Confused. Another week would pass. Events were rushing by, and his school year was coming to a close. His parents grew increasingly anxious. Now kidding, but not kidding. Where would the next meal come from? Gramps explained the concept of *"survival of the fittest"* to the family. He uttered, "Can't live on beans and hash forever. Did that back in the depression. Not a pleasant experience. And not enough nutrition in Grandma's jams and jellies to sustain a family for very long."

He folded the jacket and studied the colors for a moment. He then ambled down the steps out of the loft and, again, saw the owl peering in through the mustard-colored stained-glass window. It fixed its stare directly into his eyes.

The two dogs, still chained to a pole, yelped and barked as he carefully stepped on the pathway home, avoiding glancing in their direction.

"So, who gave you that jacket? Interesting shades of coloring. You saw the choir director again? Are you joining the choir?" His mother was on overload, asking several questions at once for Bob to digest. Plus, his headaches were getting worse.

"Yes, interesting. And, no, I'm not joining the choir. The jacket was a gift from J.J. Don't know why."

"Ah, so it's J.J. now. Rather familiar, are we? Is she befriending you? I'm sure there's something afloat with her motives. I know she's several members short with the choir. Recruitment sounds like her motive," Dad spoke up.

"Leave the boy alone, people. Maybe this J.J. is just a friendly spirit. Maybe our boy wants to learn to play that big machine. Make some noise. Right, grandson?"

Grandma added to the discussion. "I hear the church needs a thorough cleaning, and our grandson needs service hours for his scouting venture.

"I, too, say leave him alone. He'll find his own way and whatever is goin' on over there, a church no less can't be bad for the spirit," she continued, voice trailing off. Each participant parted ways. Discussion over.

4

Bob didn't sleep well over the next few days. He kept up with his studies, his paper route, his scouting, and baseball, making the varsity team.

Strange thoughts, however, hovered in his mind. These strange animals barked, howled, growled, yipped, and yapped, mouths open, red eyes glaring, all in fight mode and not backing off.

He was sick to his stomach. The headaches got worse. He thought perhaps there was some evil spell being cast on him. What crazy thoughts. Flights of fancy.

"Welcome again to my loft, lair, den of iniquity, temple in the sky. But seriously, folks. Must sit with you. Over here. No time to explain much. Glad you have the jacket on. Very important. Bags packed. Needn't fret. You're looking good the way you are."

Bob, confused, spoke awkwardly. "Just here to help the custodian clean the pews. Service hours, you know," Bob's voice trailing to a whisper.

"No, this is a bigger mission than that. Let me gather my friends."

An owl came down off a perch, inside this time, and rested on J.J.'s arm. On cue, two large dogs—the ones he saw chained

outside the church—came up to J.J. and heeled. Quiet, polite. No barking.

"Let me introduce my friends. This is Glaukes. Well-trained. Wise. All knowing. A regular encyclopedia of knowledge." His head spun toward Bob. Eyes alert. "I can communicate with him through my mind. A thought process that took both of us many years to learn. And my two canine friends, K'yon 1 and K'yon 2, are tough, but gentle. Mean-spirited, yet kind. Angry yet joyful, playful, full of energy, and youthful exuberance. Oh, but my mates have lost their masters. Glaukes longs to be back in the arms of Athena. His home is with her loving care. And my friends K'yon 1 and K'yon 2 seek their master Ares. My friends are lost souls who are now far away from their homeland. They will come with us on our quest. A quest to restore the balance in the cosmos." J.J. stopped and waited for a response.

"Where are you—we—going? What kind of quest? I'm just volunteering my time to clean up. Gotta go. Who are you really? Are you still trying to recruit me for the choir?"

"I'll explain all of it quickly. I tried to send you messages for the last month. You weren't picking up any of them. Your mind is confused. Mixed up with those animals who are out of sorts. They belong to the gods, as do my friends here. You know a lot about the history of those Greek gods. I've been chosen, and you've been selected from our fellow earthlings to make this quest—a trip with many obstacles. Our final destination is the Olympieion in Athens. The site of the Olympic gods. On the other side, we will meet Rhea, daughter of Gaia (Earth). She will lead us on our trek. We will be severely tested in the various types of love that will be shown to us. But this is no simple game.

"The Olympians are angry. They have fought each other for many millennia. The Titans in prison in Tartarus are rebelling, beginning to rise up and challenge the power of the Olympians. You must keep your jacket on at all times. Those colors hold great significance in Greek culture. Red is life and death, a coming of age. Blue represents the sky and sea in both the divine and natural world. Purple means royalty, luxury, and high status. White is all about purity, youthfulness, and feminine beauty."

"When will we return? And if we aren't successful, what will happen to us? We are just flesh and bone. I have my whole life ahead of me, preferably here on Earth with my family and friends." Bob thought this all just some fanciful story told by a flighty—he thought of the word flaky—out-of-sort storyteller with perhaps some serious emotional concerns.

Maybe she thought she could lure me into some mythical game. But where is the computer? Where is the screen set up to begin play? And the handheld controls? None to be found.

I don't think she gave me a drug to put me at her beck and call. No hypnotic state, Bob mumbling to himself. Make up your mind. He spoke. "Can I call home to tell my parents I'll be late for dinner?"

J.J. chuckled. "It's all been taken care of. You are visiting a friend. That friend has already contacted your parents. You are staying with him for a few days. His parents and your parents are okay with your visit. A few tricks of my trade. Now, no more questions."

Glaukes began flapping his wings, buzzing over J.J. and the dogs. K'yon 1 and K'yon 2 became restless. Now they were unchained and came close to Bob.

They both growled in unison, a signal to move. Bob felt as if he might be pecked at and bitten at the same time. He sensed J.J. would be in a hurry soon, running somewhere toward some, it seemed, unknown place.

5

The Quest

The time had come to make the trip. She grabbed the satchel and motioned Bob to move toward the steps. The dogs and the owl followed J.J. as she bounded down the side steps, fleeing her home away from home. Bob stumbled, caught himself, and fled to a doorway he had never seen before.

It seems to lead to a custodial closet. Once open, the vastness of space appeared before the group. They were floating, mind and body, to another place, another time. They stopped at an open field of clover, sunflowers, chrysanthemums, coronarium, wild orchids, anemones, and poppies. At an open space by a trail, they stopped. The dogs heeled. The owl rested on J.J.'s shoulder. Bob's senses were acute. He breathed, and fresh air filled his lungs with power. His eyes focused on the expanse of the open field.

A large bird hovered overhead. J.J., amused at Bob's sense of awe, said, "Oh, that's just Gy'pas, a vulture who will follow us along the way. He belongs to Ares. Yes, he's lost his master also.

"Our goal today is to reach a sanctuary several miles on this pathway. We'll rest until morning, when we will be greeted by a surprise guest who will reveal what our mission is all about, beyond what I am currently able to understand. There will be provisions there—food, a bed, maps, and instruments of all kinds. We will need to defend ourselves from time to time. There will be items we will use for those occasions." J.J. brushed some leaves off her jacket.

"Good that you still have your colored jacket on. You dressed well for the trip. At least that part I communicated to you when you were sleeping this past week."

She smiled at Bob, baring straight, white teeth, her eyes brightening and nose twitching. Her voice echoed over the top of the flowers skyward into another sphere.

"Homeric hymns. This is the Hymn to Hermes. Did you know he invented the lyre? Oh, we need to know these hymns. We will be tested.

"I will teach you the dithyrambs, lively songs of celebration. We will invoke, with these songs, the help of the gods when we need it. Her voice trailing off as the group now rambled on the pathway toward their shelter.

As they approached the site of the shelter, Bob's mind was racing. He was being transformed from a confused young boy to a young man, strong of heart and soul.

He peered skyward, and words appeared, first in Greek and then in English. The vulture had taken the clouds and formed letters, which became words of a song sung before Greek warriors took to battle:

> *"Oh, children of the Greeks, come on.*
> *Liberate the homeland, liberate also*
> *the children, the women,*
> *the altars of the gods,*
> *the tombs of your ancestors.*
> *Now is the time to fight for all."*

The sky grew dark. Pellets of rain began falling. A thunderbolt caused the angels to become startled. Several fell from the sky and came crashing onto hard ground. They lay whimpering, wings folded up, tears pouring from eyes that showed fear and trepidation.

Lightning cracked over the heads of the five travelers. The vulture, sensing danger, was intrigued and flew away to safer ground.

"Only Zeus senses our arrival. He just gets that way. Ornery, he is. He just lit up that forest over there." J.J. pointed in the direction of a mountain, the top of which was scorched and now barren.

"He is aware we are coming? Coming to what place? Why would he be concerned about us? Two dogs, an owl, a lady, and me, a teenage boy." There was no reply from J.J.

The rain ceased falling. Somehow, the group was dry. All the pellets, almost on cue, flew around them, almost as if they were being protected.

Bob started to speak again, and J.J. pointed. "There. The structure where we will be sheltered. My compass didn't let me down. Go," she commanded after unleashing the dogs. "Create a safe barrier around the dwelling."

The dogs, baring their teeth, galloped around twice. Coming back, they heeled and nodded. No hidden dangers. A safe place. Inside then. The space inside was tight, small, and almost cramped, making it difficult for all of them to fit comfortably. There was a structure to lie on, similar to a bed. There were two of these, each with a cover and blankets. Bob thought it odd that in the middle of the room, a table setting was already in place.

Food appeared on the table from nowhere. There was an assortment of fruits—figs, apples, grapes—and a pot of honey in the middle of the table. A tureen of soup made of leeks filled the air with a pleasant smell. Goat cheese and bread were on a large plate, ready to be consumed. J.J. and Bob sat across from each other. "Go on. Enjoy."

Bob questioned a cup filled with white liquid. He tasted it and winced. "Buttermilk," came the reply. It's good for the soul. Only happy cows churn it out." J.J. laughed as she downed a cup of this white liquid.

Another tray loaded with a variety of cheeses—from several locations around Greece, Bob was later told—also sat on the table.

A large oval object stared at them both from the middle of the table. "That's a quail egg. I'll cut it up. It's quite a delicacy," said J.J., reaching for a knife.

Suddenly, from a resting position, the owl went into a frenzy, wings flapping, screeching, eyes piercing, fixed on the egg.

"Oh, Glaukes, be calm. The quail is your friend in nature. This egg is a gift to be eaten by us who are human." He perched on J.J.'s shoulder, his eyes downtrodden and sad. "Well, okay, we'll just admire the gift then." The owl's eyes then lit up in approval.

"So, you can speak to this owl?" Bobby asked. "He seems to respond to your words." Bob studied J.J., looking for some measure of an answer.

"Yes, we communicate. I've known Glaukes for a few years now. He's helped me at the church with my choral group. He has perfect pitch, don't you know?"

Not knowing what to think, Bob only nodded weakly.

"But we must partake in this slab of lamb, our gesture to the gods—both the Titans and the Olympians. They are all watching us, you know. They're wondering who we are and what we're doing on their grounds, their battlefields, their territory. Humans in this part of the cosmos are a cause for much concern among these gods," she said, her voice now measured and serious. She turned to Bob. "Our business here is just beginning. Eat up. Get some rest. We have, as I said, a surprise visitor in the morning."

As he ate, he noticed the dogs lapping up some buttermilk and tearing apart pieces of the lamb. Their strength seemed to grow as the days passed. They may be getting ready for some form of battle, he thought.

The stars emerged throughout the cosmos, creating patterns in the night sky. Bobby sensed danger coming. He even thought he heard loud, crying voices imprisoned, wanting a release. But then maybe it was just his imagination, as his grandpa would say, "running away with you."

Was he asleep, or was he awake but in a dream state? The ceiling opened, and the dark sky was incredibly bright. The twinkling stars formed patterns that Bob remembered were constellations— the Great Bear (Cassiopeia), Orion, Scorpius, and Cygnus.

He felt a nudge from J.J. "Beautiful, isn't it? Vast, never-ending space. Those are the homes of bright spirits who once lived on Earth.

"The Greeks compared the cosmos to bright, shiny bronze. Those stars are the heroes and beasts praised by the Greeks. They are the mystical spirits who strode across the heavens and watched over mankind.

"But now all that watching is being upended. These spirits are practicing their dark secrets and withholding their guiding light.

"They, too, want only peace to be restored. They are thus upset at the fighting between the Titans and Olympians, even though the Titans are imprisoned. Some Titans are escaping from Tartarus."

Suddenly, the ceiling in the safe house went blank. Only the blackened paint was left.

All was still. The dogs were heard groaning as they slept. Glaukes hooted twice. His head swiveled, and his eyes were open and alert. Bob was back in a dream state, eyes shut.

6

The morning sun rushed through the panoramic window, each figure stretching to catch the rays.

J.J., energized, called out, "Up and at 'em."

From nowhere, a table appeared bearing fruit, nuts, and some type of grain in a bowl, buttermilk filling the bowl.

"We have a long journey today. Fortify yourselves." She seemed to be talking to all the creatures, including Bob.

A knock on the door came as he spilled buttermilk on his shirt. What to wear now, he thought?

A ghostlike form entered. Its parts came together as a solid to a spot at the center of the room.

It was a female form. Her feet barely touched the floor as she came into view, wearing a turret crown.

She seated herself on a large throne. The colors of the throne— red, blue, purple, and white—were familiar to all present.

On each side sat a lion, mean, ferocious, with teeth ready to strike.

A pose came to fruition. Green eyes matched green hair. A calmness filled the room.

"Welcome, you who have been chosen to come and help our ailing cosmos. You are here at my request. From the earth, you have made the journey here. Now our work begins.

"Yes, I am Rhea, Titan goddess of fertility. You know my story. I am one of the Titan gods—the goddess of motherhood

and fertility. I am mother to the Olympians.

"I am caught between two worlds. As the daughter of Gaia, I am a Titan. But now my brothers and sisters are imprisoned. They are, however, rebelling by escaping Tartarus, wreaking havoc over the countryside.

"Then, I am the mother of the Olympians. They are my children, and they, too, are rebellious, causing much trouble, especially in your world.

"Storms, pestilence, famine, families fighting against each other—all caused by my children. My plan is simple. Reach the two places where these gods gather—Mount Olympus and Thessaly, near Mt. Othrys, where the Titans gather—located just a few kilometers apart.

"We will meet both sides in the middle and will use our wisdom and all the knowledge in the cosmos at our disposal to create peace, love, and mutual understanding, as engaging in senseless warfare just leads to more chaos, divisiveness, and the illusion of one side being in the right and the other side in the wrong.

"Our words must be matched with love and a commitment to help each side find lasting peace.

"Along our journey, we must find and exemplify the eight ways of loving and expressions of kindness.

"You, Bob, J.J., even K'yon one and two, and Glaukes have been taught these loving ways. Ergo, why you have been brought to these parts.

"Gy'pas will also guide you. He seeks to find his master, Ares, and return to his homeland.

"Upon arriving at our destination, we will be greeted by Peristora the dove and Kuknos the swan, emblems of peace, who will be by our side when facing the gods.

"I have prophesied we will ultimately meet Zeus, leader of the Olympians, and Cronus, leader of the Titans, in the middle of their respective homes. They will, if allowed, kill each other using their god given powers.

"Don't mean to ignore you, J.J. We meet again. You have been a faithful servant of Gaia, the earth goddess, maintaining her beauty and natural splendor.

"So, you've found employment practicing your faith, playing your music, turning non-believers into believers, and teaching the truths of our several varieties of love.

"But now you, too, know all too well our plight.

"You have brought the boy along as an innocent believer in his faith, yet still growing in the divine tradition of the Christian ways.

"Yes, you earthlings believe in just one god. However, you are familiar with the Greek traditions of loving and caring for one another. That part of our story is real, passed down to you, and not just a myth.

"The gods are watching our every move. We must be careful in how we proceed. I see you have the case containing weapons that you—we—may have to use on our way. They are of a small size in the case, but upon taking them out, they expand to full size. You and Bob both have a spear, or dory, a slinger, a sword, and a shield.

"I see you have found the proper dress for protection. We will encounter a few regular Greek soldiers, or hoplites, who will make our passage difficult.

"Oh yes, my two lion friends are harmless creatures; they are very tame. They cannot but wouldn't harm a fly. Useless in battle, they are strictly ornamental.

"K'yon 1 and K'yon 2 will indeed be helpful. So, J.J., you have brought all the ingredients for our quest—wisdom, strength, innocence of youth, inquisitiveness, and the central power of feminine wiles.

Finally, a moment of serene tranquility. A blush of a type of mild serenity overcame all who were present in this moment.

J.J. spoke up to the goddess. Glaukes was perched on her shoulder, and the dogs, teeth barred for a fight, stared up at the lions. Rhea's image seemed to disappear then reappear and was hazy at best.

"You have given our mission a purpose. If we, who are great of spirit and heart, can help you bring peace among the gods here and on Earth, then we can prosper from our venture, and it will be a start toward everyone's salvation. A mighty chore at best. Let's get started."

Bob started to speak, but held himself in. *How,* he thought, *does J.J. know this Rhea person? And I was chosen because of my youthful innocence. Whatever that means.*

The doors opened. In an instant, everyone was outside. Rhea led the way. "Catch up. Follow me. The path is just ahead."

Bob peered back over his shoulder where the safe house had disappeared. Vanished into thin air. Where would the next safe-house be?

The countryside had many twists and turns. They came upon a large body of water. Rhea motioned everyone to stop in their tracks. "He is angry. He watches our every move."

Suddenly, a dolphin appeared off in the distant waters of the sea. It made a shrieking noise, and its upper body started shaking in a playful pose.

"Go, Bob, use your innocent nature. Make some high-pitched sounds. Dance wildly on the beach and flail your arms joyfully," Rhea coaxed.

Reluctantly, he did as he was told. He felt a certain embarrassment, a foolish sensation causing him to blush.

This group was now reacting to his unlike posture. From a quiet, shy boy to a twisting, turning, laughing young boy.

Glaukes flew to his shoulder, sat, wriggled his torso, and made what sounded like an off-key hoot. The owl posted a wizened smile, something hard to accomplish for such a creature.

K'yon 1 and K'yon 2 were up on their hind legs, twirling in circles. Could it be they spoke a gurgle of laughter? They were not snarling.

Even the lions moved lyrically in a state of frivolity, no longer appearing as statues for Rhea.

J.J. and Rhea smiled and whispered to each other. J.J. first. "Back in our time, when the earth expressed its joy. More than smiles. Contagious, isn't it?"

Rhea was shimmering. Her multi-colored outfit, making her regal in appearance, changed in tone. Rays of bright light were cast toward the dolphin.

The dolphin understood this tone, knowing it was a message to deliver to Poseidon.

Rhea stopped her shimmering; then, she spoke. "My message to Poseidon is to stay calm and let the seas become tranquil. Let the creatures of the deep proceed unabated by your tumultuous ways. Pray and connect to the other gods. So be it. Start now."

The sun shone. For now, the seas were calm. Even the lapping sound from waves coming onto the beach ceased to be heard.

"We have met the first challenge. A kind of joyful, playful love we have given Poseidon. This ludus form has been cast out to him and all the creatures of the sea. Let us continue our journey. The pathway ahead calls us."

Everyone followed Rhea, and the procession came upon a crusty, rocky, stone-infested trail.

Both dogs yelped as small pebbles became lodged in their padded feet. The lions floated next to Rhea, unencumbered by the creatures having to walk.

The trail turned upward and zigzagged. Suddenly, pebbles flew down at the walkers below. Then some large rocks. Then boulders. "Hurry, into that cave," he heard J.J.'s voice demand. The group made it safely into the orifice.

Rhea shouted out, "This is Zeus's doing. Giving us a scare by using his Hundred-handers to carry out his mission of chaos and fear."

Glaukes flew off J.J.'s shoulder and headed for the chief of the Handers.

"Ah, our wise one will take care of this predicament. He will speak in the language of the Hander to clear the pathway for our continued journey." J.J. smiled, knowing this brief encounter was but one misstep, and a long trip was still ahead.

But then the sky became darkened. Lightning split trees on the pathway. Fires erupted in a forest just off the path, just ahead of the cave.

Bob crouched in fear, his young mind thinking the worst was yet to come.

J.J. and Rhea both summoned their powers of tranquility and divine peace. The winds stopped howling. The lightning subsided. Everyone in the cave could hear and feel each other's breathing, their hearts now in a calming mode.

A warm breath of fresh air passed over the group. All became silent for several earthly minutes.

Glaukes came back and landed on J.J.'s shoulder. He hooted and seemed to holler strange sounds—a whooshing, cooing, screeching, clamoring, clatter of unrecognizable tones and pitches. Finally, it seemed to reach a final utterance, and all sighed with relief.

Then, exhausted, Bob slumped down and closed his eyes, drifting off to sleep. All the figures gathered around Rhea for an explanation. "Oh, wise Glaukes, you have negotiated a peace with the Handers. I know you and the Handers go back many millennia. You used to guide and teach them practical ways to live and respect each soul that came into their presence.

"Now Zeus has corrupted them. He has sent them on missions of destruction. But now you have shown your pragma and enduring love to make them see and experience the many errors in their ways.

"This makes another type of love we have come across. Our pathway is again cleared for our continued journey.

"Let us stay here this night and begin our journey anew in the morning. No need to use our warring munitions."

From the surrounding fields, the many species of birds brought figs, olives, and edible roots to a set place outside the cave. A jug of wine was set in the middle. A minor feast to take place, to be sure.

At the end of the meal, J.J. took Bob aside. "Before we depart in the morning, I will impart an important message to you, which you will remember as we trek farther toward Mt. Othrys and Mt. Olympus."

Bob did not sleep well. He was up in the middle of the night, leaving the comfort of the cave for an instant, peering up at the sky above, trying to trace the patterns of the stars. Naming the constellations as the Greeks had created. His mind was numb. This journey for him was more confusing and caused him to feel more pressure on his temples.

He thought he felt a breath of moving, warm air pass by his face, and suddenly he was asleep.

7

"From now on, you're on your own. Neither Rhea nor I will be guiding you, telling you, or insisting you do something our way. Are you looking at me when I'm talking?" J.J.'s stern look betrayed her usual informal ways up to now.

Bob, sand in eyes, yawning, turned to J.J. and simply got off a weak, "What did you say?"

"Use force when necessary. Open up your case. Take out the shield, the sword, the slingers if you feel you must, but I will only tell you to use your words most of the time."

Rhea floated by the group now assembling at the cave opening. "The next pathway lies ahead."

The troop began another day in unison, following Rhea and J.J. on a road that narrowed as it wound through the Grecian countryside.

Bob's mind wandered. He told himself there must be some plan here and now. He knew he must stay out of trouble and away from danger. This seemed to be the easy part. His mind, however, couldn't account for what dangers might be lurking ahead.

What did J.J. mean she and Rhea weren't going to tell him what to do anymore? Weren't they the adults? Surely, they should know the dangers of this trip.

And what if they met a large group of hoplites? Would they be peaceful? What were those people like? If they were formed to

protect Zeus, he assumed they wouldn't be friendly.

"Break here," commanded Rhea, showing no physical stress.

"I have made friends with an archangel. All the angels in this region have begun to understand our mission. We now need the eight other categories to comply and take sides in our fight."

Suddenly, a mid-afternoon feast was laid out on an open area amongst the most beautiful flowers and plants Bob had ever seen.

Bob felt a whooshing sensation brushing his face, similar to what he felt when he fell asleep the previous night.

His mood changed from doubt—some fear and anxiety—to wanting to laugh, a feeling of semi-joy, he thought to himself.

All was calm. Rhea, now above the group, seemed to spread her form in many directions. She appeared hazy, yet certain colors—the colors of the coat Bob and J.J. were wearing—shone brightly across the afternoon sky.

In the far distance, Bob viewed an enormous figure. It was the shape of a man. Closer he came. Now in full view.

He appeared mad, angry, exhausted, and frustrated. These were the only words Bob could figure out from his limited vocabulary. A roar blasted the air.

"Zeus. A not-so-fair punishment. I was a leader. Banished was I. Battle lost. My fellow Titans in Tartarus. Now escaping. Zeus will be brought to justice soon."

Looking down at a singular figure still holding up the heavens, he spoke. "Who are you? What are you doing here? This territory is for the gods. I know by your frail presence you are a mere human animal."

Bob reacted cautiously, then spoke in soft whispers: "I know you from Greek mythology. You are Atlas, holding up the heavens. Quite a burden, I would say. You fought bravely, leading your men and the Titans into battle, but Zeus defeated your army. You must be very tired. I heard the word *weary* once. That's it. You look *weary*."

Atlas focused on this object below. "So, you've read about me and know about my abilities in battle. Leader of men, I say." He was now straining even harder, his shoulders aching now more than ever.

But, my little human soul, what are you doing here? There is no space or time here. Come to think of it, there is no here either.

A clamminess drenched Bob. Currents of warm air brushed his face, creating a tingling sensation from head to toe.

He looked behind him with hopes of getting some support from J.J., Rhea, the owl, and even the dogs to growl. Be fierce guard dogs, K'yon 1 and 2.

But there was no one behind him, or anywhere else for that matter.

Atlas spoke one last time. "So, I will answer my question. All of us are watching you and your procession. You are here to defeat our enemy, Zeus, and his Olympian army. Join us in battle, dear friend. Take my pain away. Our troops will support you and your troop anyway we can."

Bob's brows dropped. He collapsed to his knees. Frightened, alone in this wilderness, he spoke a new truth he didn't understand:

"No, my friends and I are on this mission to find a solution to all your fighting. Revenge is not the answer. We come in peace. I am only a mere mortal, as you say, a young mortal new to the ways of my world or your world."

With those words, the heavens exploded. Lightning struck the ground in several places around Bob. Zeus took note.

"Then your flesh will burn, and your life will end as you beings know it. Don't you hear Zeus now? His power rules the cosmos."

Atlas turned and faded through a curtain of smoke. The smell of burning flesh filled the air.

Bob was left kneeling. His own flesh quivering. The headaches became more intense. Where was his own troop of soldiers? Was he now officially on some battlefield? He didn't use any of his weapons from the case he was given.

Suddenly, the heavens opened up and the winds uprooted some trees. Torrents of rain spread through the countryside.

He closed his eyes, and sleep came upon him. When he opened them, he saw the countryside blooming with a splendor of colors—again, all the colors from the coat he was wearing.

"Welcome back, dear boy." He was face-to-face with J.J., her teeth sparkling. She looked younger than he remembered, though his memory was fading back in time. No time. Here, there, everywhere. Confusion. Headaches remain.

"Your youth here was an example of your innocence. You displayed no hatred. You were on your own. Alone.

"We are moving closer to our goal. Rhea will explain where we are with our journey."

J.J. sat down by Bob. The animals moved in to form a circle around Bob. Rhea appeared from behind a foggy cloud, her form taking shape. All was still, and a calm filled the air. When she spoke, all creatures within earshot stopped what they were doing to listen: "Our journey so far has taken many forms," Rhea spoke softly. "We are now a family united in our brethren ways. We each have a role to play in our quest. Young Bob here just expressed a type of love for Atlas and his plight. A love of affection and respect, *phillis* to the Greeks. But we must move on. Stay close to each other along this upcoming narrow pathway." The lions immediately nestled next to Rhea. They appeared to be sleeping, faking a yawn, but ready to battle if needed.

K'yon 1 and 2 again bared their teeth. A guttural growl emerged from deep in their throats. Glaukes became very active, flapping its wings. An expression of aggression appeared on its face, taking the place of its usual calm, wise ways.

What was stirring up these hostile images? J.J. wanted to interrupt Rhea, but she let her finish. "Again, I know the gods are following our every move. Zeus, especially, is calling on all his powers to push us back, to do away with us, or even to chain us in the prison at Tartarus."

The group huddled together as they trekked up a mountainside path. Fog filled the air, and a smell of burnt timber created fumes, making it hard for these travelers to breathe. The animals began gasping for air, pure air, but none was available.

J.J., Rhea, and Bob together decided that they all needed to find a place of comfort to rest and to escape these fumes.

A bright light shone ahead off the side of the mountain in a valley below.

"There—let's move our family toward that light." J.J., now in

the lead, broke into a gliding stride. The rest followed.

"Stop here," she ordered and motioned for everyone to gather together. They saw a fire pit where someone was sitting and warming themselves. "I'll proceed cautiously."

A few feet away from the figure, she was suddenly startled and let out a loud, raucous laugh. "It's you, my friend!"

A large, bearded man sat precariously in tattered clothes with a disheveled demeanor, hands cupped, leaning over the fire for warmth, alone on this chilly, dark night.

"Prometheus, you're free. But alone here. The great humanitarian. A focus of divine love and truth."

The two bodies faced each other. A grin; then a chuckle; then another burst of laughter from J.J.

The other figure, coming more into view, recognized his friend. His sad eyes opened, and his mouth turned up into a slight grin. "You're here. Back home on your soil. Human, but much more than that—a true patriot," he said, his mind drifting.

The others finally caught up with J.J.. They gathered around the pit, curious as to who this new creature really was.

Rhea floated over the pit, careful not to be burned. Her farm surrounded this stranger, who was a friend to J.J. from many eras past.

"The story to be told. Sit everyone around the pit. Glaukes rested on J.J.'s shoulder. K'yon 1 and 2 heeled at the foot of J.J. Even the vulture took time to stop his hovering overhead. Bob nestled closer to J.J. He felt her strength of heart and mind taking over this proceeding.

"My loving, caring friend fought hard against Zeus. He is a Titan. He and the army of the Titans lost. You were chained, but

Heracles (Hercules) freed you because Zeus needed you to find the apples of Hesperides. That would aid Zeus' son.

"You also knew a secret that if Zeus marries Nereid Thetis, she will bear a son who will overthrow his father.

"So, you and Zeus reconciled. You came over to the side of the Olympians, and thus peace spread throughout the cosmos for many eons.

"But let me tell you why we two are loving, caring friends.

Tears welled up in J.J.'s eyes. Prometheus's face emitted a bright red tone brought on by his own body heat, not that contained in the fire pit.

"Remember when you raided the workshop of Hephaestus and Athena on Mt. Olympus and stole fire?

"You gave this gift to mankind and allowed mankind to keep warm, cook food, and forge metals.

"The human populations moved ahead in civilizing themselves, and you helped create many advances in their health and well-being and in making life better for all creatures below."

"Wait. No more of this talk. Don't spread these words of destruction to your little group here." Prometheus's face reddened even more. A scowl blanketed his face.

"So I gave humanity the gift of fire. And what do these humans do? They build explosives. Enough to kill all of their civilization. And why do millions of those humans lack enough food to sustain their bodies?

"You tell me, J.J. I sit here, now unbound, willing to help our gods and humans alike, yet I feel useless. We should band together as brethren. Solutions come as like minds combine their expertise to create new pathways along the trail to successful outcomes."

"Stop right there," Janina responded quickly. "You made it possible for mankind to advance. Whatever mankind does with the gift is up to them. Don't blame yourself for the decisions humans make."

"Just tell me," Prometheus went on. "If I'm so good for mankind, why am I sitting here around a fire pit with flames bursting and destroying the forest below? Why does climate change the landscape both here and below? You and Gaia are helpless to stop the carnage."

"Again, I say you have provided mankind with these tools, yet they still have to decide their fate. Free will, Prometheus. Free will."

J.J. dropped to her knees in a pleading position. My old friend, let us rejoice this evening. A meal around the pit for all of us to partake in. A dance for all of us gathered here. Remember those days we danced the syrtos, the chain dance? Remember, too, Terpsichore, one of the nine muses, patrons of lyric poetry and dancing at each of our events.

"Those were good times for outweighing the tragedies. You, with your kindness and blessings to your fellow gods and all of mankind below."

"For one evening then. You and your little band of warriors who are here on some quest, getting closer to the—maybe for you—tragic action," said Prometheus, relenting to this request.

A long banquet table appeared from the ground. Lamb, vegetables, and assorted desserts filled the tabletop.

J.J. and Prometheus sat close to each other. Bob, also next to

J.J., was perplexed by J.J.'s show of emotion. Was she becoming frustrated on this trip with this motley crew of soldiers?

He sensed she was very close to Prometheus. What great adventures both must have experienced together in past times.

"The chain dance it is. Each of the animals lined up around the pit at J.J.'s command. The dogs and lions up on two legs began hopping around the pit. Glaukes rested on J.J.'s shoulder and began a stutter step.

J.J., Bob, and Prometheus hooked up arm in arm and, in a rhythmic fashion, paraded around the pit.

"Look up there," J.J. said, pointing skyward. "An angel of principality. The angel who guards kingdoms and communities. We are blessed this evening.

"Even Zeus cannot penetrate this angel's holy veil. This angel will lead us safely to our destination. One can only hope this to be the case."

Rhea was hovering, shimmering over the proceedings, calm as usual. She spoke to the group: "And dear ones, we have met the standards for the ways of expressing love. Prometheus has shown us his hospitality. He has given us the love of Xenia. His welcoming, unconditional love to us who are travelers in his region of the cosmos. He has also shown his charity by providing a modern sense of altruism. Prometheus, you sense the good in all creatures below and even the gods here who are fighting among themselves. This is a form of agape love, a love that has always existed and now needs to be restored among all beings and gods. A chore, to be sure, but one in which our little band of warriors is engaged. We welcome Prometheus' love and support even from afar."

Tears rolled down his cheeks, splashing into the fire pit, but the flames were not extinguished.

He spoke briefly: "Go, my brethren. Face the ultimate challenge. Let your hearts swell with all the kinds of love necessary to overpower the evil-doers you are sure to face once you reach your ultimate destination."

Everyone collapsed, exhausted as the dancing ceased. Animals and humans alike fell asleep under the stars. Morning came all too soon, and once again the band of soldiers marched on, following J.J. and Rhea across a massive field exhibiting a variety of flora and fauna.

"Those olive trees are the size of skyscrapers. These oak, rowan, and maple have grown bigger than any I have seen. Those orchids carry all the colors of rainbows ever produced by the gods.

"Look over there, Bob. Those clumps of forest are the mystic trees and the carob trees. On the side of that cliff," said J.J., pointing, "are cliff roses—hardy survivors in all kinds of weather. And those purple flowers—" J.J. gasped, motioning for Bob to sit on a boulder as the rest of the crew suddenly halted, "—those purple flowers are hyacinths. Once there lived a beautiful Spartan youth. He had the potential to be a great warrior but was tragically killed in battle. The god Apollo, who loved this youth, spilled Hyacinthus's blood onto a flower. He called it a hyacinth.

"To this day, the flower is a cry of sorrow. Those who gaze upon these flowers can remember and grieve as a remembrance of loved ones who have died—either in battle or of natural causes.

"For me, at that time, wars had broken out all over the cosmos. I was helping nurse those wounded soldiers.

"It was a time in my life, my youth, that I admired those soldiers. I thought they were my heroes. I thought once one side won, the cosmos would be a better place.

"I was wrong. The wars continued with no positive outcome. I still wondered if I should choose a side?

"Then, as chance would have it, I met Apollo. His intense love gave me hope that better times were ahead.

"He taught me his knowledge of music, poetry, light, prophecy, and healing. He was associated with the sun and truth.

"Our love was of Eros—passionate, romantic, powerful, and intense. Though I was still very young, I grew and matured into a fully grown entity capable of teaching others what those traits were all about.

"Over marked time, whole civilizations have come and gone. Each succeeding state, over time, succumbs to the excesses of power, greed, and corruption and fails to abide by what Apollo and other gods in previous times have instructed the world below—that there are five creeds to follow, creating a lasting peace.

"Inspiration, knowledge, reason, protection, and purification—thought out and practiced can sustain a civilization over a long period of marked time.

"But now the gods themselves are fighting each other. I know what our mission is to be, but I will admit I am frightened."

"Enough of your rummaging nature," said Rhea, now hovering over the group. "We are all here to serve a purpose, and we are engaging that purpose and confronting our fears.

"Move on, everyone. Lions by my side. Glaukes, be wise. Instruct J.J. of your positive instinctual ways. K'yon 1 and 2, keep your battle armor on. Prepare the way ahead with your pure sense of smell, telling us of dangers to come.

"And, Bob, use your innocence and youth to confront the evil ahead."

The procession marched in lockstep through the rest of the immense array of fauna and flowers.

At the edge, J.J. motioned for them to stop. Tall yellow flowers, endless rows and rows stretching for another acre or so, stared menacingly at the group. "Daffodils!" J.J. shrieked, dropping to her knees. They are a symbol of death—evil is upon us!"

And they continued to march. They gathered on a firm pathway to continue their trek.

After walking for miles, J.J. spotted a large building, temple-like with columns surrounding the structure, a display of Ionic and Doric architecture. Windows allowed the light to filter into the inside. It was a perfect three-by-five design. J.J., talking to herself, knew most Greek structures adhered to this mathematical formula.

Suddenly, from behind a stone structure, several objects emerged in full combat gear, charging full speed toward the group.

"Halt! Cease your movement and stand in one place!" Their leader approached J.J. Several other soldiers surrounded the group.

"Quiet, K'yon 1 and 2." She put her hand on the dogs' shoulders. Glaukes fluttered aimlessly. He peered skyward and noticed the vulture, which had made the trip to this point, dive toward the ground, barely landing in an upright position just short of the front steps.

A figure from inside emerged, clothed in a toga and sandals. "Friends or foes, welcome to my country retreat. Bring these visitors to me." He motioned to the chief hoplite.

The crew was ushered into a massive foyer. Light shone through the windows in all directions, reflecting these rays of light.

Oh, let us all go to my gardens to welcome you. The hoplites placed their spears on each individual. There were places for each to sit by a pool filled with fronds, water lilies, and large carp.

"I see we have a famous visitor. Rhea—my fair lady. Welcome to my retreat. I see you have brought your usual odd assortment of characters on what—another mission of peace, my dear?"

"Oh, how you keep trying to quell the gods. Let them alone, dear girl."

Rhea knew who this being was—or rather who this god was.

J.J., too, knew she was in the presence of a famous Olympian. Her disposition changed from awe to anger, her face reddening, now knowing she may be a prisoner in this marbled castle.

"Yes, so you have wandered into our territory. You never give up trying to promote some form of peace, do you?

"Oh, Rhea, my dear Rhea, or should I say *grandmother*." A gasp was heard around the room.

Bob tried to piece together his memory of what gods were related to whom and why, but somehow this connection failed to register.

J.J. knew the lineage but didn't know Rhea was now being deliberate in searching out this Olympian. She now felt betrayed by Rhea. This was an unexpected stop before they reached their final destination.

"So, you have sought me out? And why? Your so-called peace-loving ways don't fool me. You have given birth to many children. I would say most of those who were and are very vengeful. Tell me then that you had the influence—you and Cronus, the grandfather—to raise us up as kind, gentle souls.

"You should know by now, we who are gods thirst for power. What is peace anyway but the lull between battles? In battle, our divine souls are at their best, finding an enemy to slay, people to conquer, territory to annex, and reasons to breathe fires of damnation."

"Enough of your outbursts." Rhea now positioned herself on a table directly across from Ares, her turreted crown throwing darts of electric shock across at him. Her celestial garment flamed reds, yellows, and purple, shooting these colors in all directions, making the area light up, turning a sunrise into a sunset.

"The past is done. We only have our present, and we can hope for peace in the eons to come."

"I laugh at your poor attempt to convince me that peace is an option in any way, shape, or form in the cosmos. As we speak, those Titans are rising up, some escaping from Tartarus. We are marshalling our soldiers to destroy those poor souls. And you, with your pathetic band of creatures, actually desire to come between our two mighty forces. How dare you have the audacity to venture here and challenge even one iota of our right to defend our part of the cosmos and to rule over those who challenge our ways and values."

Rhea started to express an angry response, but remained calm in her reply: "So what has fighting these battles of yours ever proved? You fought in the Trojan War and switched to the

Greek side. Quite a convenient switch from losers to winners. You fought in the battle of Gigantomachy and were defeated by Heracles. You were wounded by Diomedes, a Greek hero. And then you had a battle with Athena and were wounded by her. Wouldn't you say, summing up, your performances on the field of battle were, to say the least, not up to Greek standards? Very poor indeed."

"Oh, Grandma, always the critic. Not up to your standards, I say. So, you see, you, too, can be brutal in an assessment of your own family, a grandson no less. So, where is your love and kindness? You come to my retreat all shimmering and glowing with your message of kindness and love, and accuse me of being brutal on and off the battlefield. Let me get this straight, dear Grandma—my father, your son, is the most brutal of all the gods, Titans, or Olympians. He hears your every pitiful cry to "put down your arms" and seek peace and love. We can be a family again. Get real. The battlefield is where real love is practiced. Eliminate your opposition, and peace and tranquility will follow."

Rhea pleaded again: "You had your chance for love and peace in domesticity with Aphrodite. You had it all. But to no avail. You spent your days planning for war and becoming a bloodthirsty butcher on the field of battle. Aphrodite told you she would make a home for you and any children you might have. Again, you chose the path of war.

"Instead, she sought the love of Hephaestus, god of the forge. He is a loving, caring craftsman, a truly creative man."

"So, Grandma, you have brought this sickly band of weak-minded, soul-searching do-nothings this far along our bumpy mountainous trails. And to what end? To be slaughtered as they arrive at Mt. Olympus and Mt. Othrys.

"You, as a goddess, may survive at that point, but your earthling friends will surely be consumed in the frenzied activity.

"Two great powers meeting. We, the Olympians, must certainly survive and drive the Titans once again back to their prison home in Tartarus."

All the while, J.J., Bob, and the animals sat watching and listening to the two adversaries go at it. J.J. knew the trip from this point on would be more treacherous than ever. She now had reservations and doubts that this tiny band of soldiers could affect the outcome—or even have any influence when it came to providing some type of peace in the cosmos.

She now didn't know what motivated Rhea to even want to lead this small band made up of animals and humankind.

It seemed odd to J.J. that eons ago these same Greek gods ruled mankind, affecting every aspect of the Greeks' lives. Now the gods are destroying each other, as mankind may likewise, but is struggling with the idea—no more wars.

And who should be chosen to face these gods? she thought. *A young boy—pubescent no less—and myself, a human, too, but one with a divine nature who knows the portal system to even enter this world of the gods.*

Rhea has led us up to this point, but I wonder how much further we can go with her into the battlegrounds.

Those thoughts vanished as Ares retook center stage. "So, we will all feast this evening in the cool air here in our terraced garden setting. Off to battle, you band of lost souls."

A long table was brought onto the patio. Servants served portions of lamb, fruits, nuts, olives, and local produce.

The sun set. J.J., Bob, Glaukes, and K'yon 1 and 2 bed down in separate rooms in the mansion. Rhea floated to another room with the two lions always at her side.

Ares and his troops slept in his quarters at the back of the estate. Ares was happy that Gy'pas, his pet vulture, had returned to his rightful owner.

At least Ares thought something good came from this sudden, intrusive trip brought about by his grandmother's presence.

8

The morning air was crisp, calm, and refreshing for all the travelers. Before they ventured back on their pathway, J.J. thought it best to briefly discuss with Bob the dangers he is bound to face both along this final stretch and the unknown once reaching their ultimate destination.

"Sit down over here." Bob complied. "So, we are heading toward our final destination. What we will find is unknown. So far, you have been a passive visitor at every turn of an event. But you have not panicked. You have not used your armaments so far in any kind of battle. You have kept your coat of colors on every moment so far. You have been kind, even playful, to my dogs. You have let Glaukes and his wisdom guide us on this voyage. You have let Rhea state her case, knowing she has given birth to Zeus, Hades, Hera, Hestia, and Demeter. You were selected by a committee made up of Olympian and Titan goddesses. These Titan goddesses are Theia, goddess of light; Themus, goddess of divine law; Mnemosyne, goddess of memory; Phoebe, goddess of prophecy and intellect; and Tethys, goddess of rivers and oceans. They will be guiding you throughout your journey, some of which will be arduous, heart-wrenching, and soul-searching."

"Wait a minute," Bob interrupted. "Why are you telling me all this? Isn't everyone coming along? We're all together, right? Family, right?" Bob, face now flushed, head bowed, knees weak and shaking, posed the only thought to enter his mind.

"Where am I going and why? So, am I being used for some experiment? Why, J.J., have you brought me here? You say I have been chosen, but to do what? I'm aware the gods are angry. The two forces are clashing. They're out to destroy each other. I know I'm the human one here. I can pinch myself and feel the pain. And who are you anyway? Some person, divine or not, into the business of saving souls? Your music at the church, your singing—I've never seen you down from that loft. Do you have another life? Friends? Family? A marriage?"

J.J. cut him off. "All in due time. But let me warn you. All the stages except one have been achieved. You must step up and fill in the last one—philautia. This one is seen as self-love. You must love yourself and what you are doing. To you, it may appear to be self-centeredness.

"Regardless of the event or situation, you must be strong. You must appear to be joyful, forthright, and very sure of yourself—"

Bob cut in: "Or what might happen?" Now his knees shook even more. His throat tightened. He was light-headed. His stomach churned.

J.J. replied: "I don't know. All I know is we have a path to walk. All of us. We will come to a fork. You will pick one. One will be the safe way and one fraught with danger. We will separate. You will go one way, the rest of us the other. I had been foretold by the supreme power in the cosmos that this would be the case. And now we are here. Then let us go." The group of warriors began on another path. This time Bob led the way.

"Move closer to me," Bob chirped. "Stay together. Glaukes, get back on J.J.'s shoulder. Why are you flapping all over the place?

"Where is Rhea? Floating on her own in space somewhere.

There's one lion running across a meadow. How do I get his attention? And J.J. seemed to be way back with her dogs. Pick up the pace, please. K'yon 1, or was it K'yon 2—Bob was never able to tell them apart—was following and barking at some strange-looking creature that had bounced into the meadow alongside the road. Both animals could no longer be seen."

Bob was frustrated trying to account for his team as other thoughts raced through his mind.

Who were these female goddesses whom J.J. said chose him for this journey? Indeed, something J.J. made up to make him feel important. Well, it didn't work, he told himself. *He felt totally lost out here, or wherever we are.*

Did time stand still? Days and nights seemed to be running together. He could still view the vast array of constellations on those clear, dark nights. He felt the hot rays of the sun burn into his skin during these hazy, he supposed, summer days.

His diet was kept up—natural food from area meadows and lamb in many forms. He felt his physical body expanding even with all this trudging and walking.

But he had a sense of drifting way back in his own perceived definition of time. J.J., his best friend on this trip, would tell him he is "soul searching." For what? To what extent? And why? He had no clue.

The little band suddenly fell back in line. Maybe hours of walking. The sun is at its apex in the sky. Time to rest. Some food to eat. Take a break.

J.J. broke the silence, "We've arrived. This is the fork in the road. Here we are. Bob, over here. Address the group. You have a choice to make."

It was J.J.'s voice that drew everyone together. Bob stood at the apex of the divide, peering down two long roads. Both narrowed in scope.

He took a deep breath and made his announcement. "I have chosen this left side. I'm sure it will lead me to our final destination. I'm sure you will also have a safe trip." He was not too sure which way was treacherous. Was he leaving his family here to go safely, or was he going into the unknown, into dangerous territory?

His final steps were small. His stride became longer as he gained momentum. This part of the path was wide, unencumbered, easy going.

He realized he never looked back at all the characters he had come to know and, yes, come to love. He still had many questions as to how he arrived here in this strange land, or cosmos, as it was explained to him. And why this solo journey? The rest of the way to what he supposed was the great battlefield—Titans versus Olympians.

He was also thinking about this last form of the ways the Greeks expressed love—philautia, or self-love.

I like myself, he thought, *but do I love myself? What would it mean to really be in love with oneself?*

His family members at home always told him to think of others first, not yourself. They went to church to pray for others first. His father had expressions like, "Son, get off your high horse—who do you think you are?"

Another expression he heard from his father to his mother was, Our son is too big for his britches, meaning he thinks he's better than he really is.

So now, according to J.J., I have to promote myself and be the center of attention. He heard the term bragging. He wondered if that was what being self-centered was all about. And was that a good thing?

Now these thoughts were overtaken by the pangs in his stomach. He was told by J.J. that along these routes, no matter which one was chosen, he would find berries, herbs, and nuts to live on. Up to this point, he found little to be called food. He was told he was close to the final destination anyway, so perhaps a few more miles would be enough distance, a mild inconvenience at best. So, he must think of a strategy to use when facing these gods of war.

Surely his friends would meet him at some point soon, and they would all come up with a similar strategy that could be applied. A peaceful, non-lethal, diplomatic peace. Especially for Rhea. She was a very important goddess who birthed Zeus. Indeed, as a mother, she could find a way to make him stop his brutality.

He was now beginning to be more at ease with his thoughts. He did, at this point, like himself more for paying attention to this role he was playing.

But the pathway never seemed to end. He was beginning to find brambles and debris on the road. At first, he brushed it aside, then he had to stop for a few minutes and pick up limbs that impeded his journey. The sky darkened after what seemed like many hours of walking, and darkness chilled the air. There were no constellations in this evening's sky. Not one star twinkled. He was wearing his coat of many colors, which, to him, strangely enough kept him warm.

How he would find food in the dark, he was not sure. There were many trees along the pathway, but all, it seemed, were bare. It was as if someone or something had hacked away and rendered these trees and bushes lifeless.

Suddenly, the wind changed direction, and the smell of stench was in the air. That of rotten flesh. He covered his mouth and nose. Now his eyes watered. His head was throbbing worse than ever. The pain of a thousand nails pierced his temples, and sweat dribbled off his coat from his face, which had reddened and turned blotchy with brown patches of skin breaking out. His limbs felt weak. His legs seemed as if they were cast in stone. The arms fell awkwardly off his shoulders. His fingers grew numb.

Dropping to all fours, he tried to maintain his balance but soon lay prostrate, unable to move a muscle. However, they kept twitching in a spasmodic fashion.

The sky grew darker than ever, or was it just this being succumbing to some unknown force now beginning to take his life away?

The boat was rocking. A figure was steering ever so gently. "Ah, I see your eyes are in the present. You are being ferried by Charon. I have been described as a malodorous ogre, a grumpy old man just doin' my job.

"We are going across the river Styx. This is the river of hate. Your punishment will be determined when you get to the other side." He looked at the figure with him in the boat.

"A young lost soul this one. It's anyone's guess as to where you'll end up. Get out now. Off with you. Someone will be here soon. But what is time to you? At least you were a light load. Gotta go fetch more lost souls."

The boy in the boat flopped onto shore, water splashing his backside. He waited in the dark. No one came for what seemed like a long time. But as Charon said, "What is time anyway?"

His eyes adjusted to the darkness in the room. Rays of light shone through a window. Stained-glass, he surmised.

Sitting on a tall hardback chair caused him some discomfort, but his mind took over. Some confusion mixed with anger overcame his fear as to who or what these people, creatures, were who were apparently holding him hostage.

Ahead of where he was seated, up high, almost to the ceiling, was a balcony. Several seats were in place across a long table-like structure.

"Can you hear me down there? Unshackle him." It was then that this person noticed the young man was not bound. Nor was there a gag over his mouth.

"About your punishment."

It was at this moment two other elderly men whispered in the first one's ear. "He's a live one. Down here for instructions. You know, Minos, we're just beginning to provide this service to those above now. Compliments of the new regime."

"Ah, yes, but this bureaucracy is tiring me out. So many changes over these past few eons."

Minos continued to address the subject down below in front of him: "So, a history lesson it is. Then to your punishment."

Again, the two others whispered in his ear. "Well, yes, yes, I'll keep an open mind. So be it. Just when I was used to all that torment. Okay, so where were we? You crossed the river Styx, the river of hate, and there are four more rivers you could have crossed—the Acheron, river of woe; the Cocytus, river of lamentation; the Lethe, river of forgetfulness; and the Phlegethon, river of fire. Quite a variety, wouldn't you say? Oh, and after death, we three—Rhadamanthus, Aeacus, and I—decide your soul's fate. Peaceful souls rest at Elysian. Those souls that are at relative peace go to the Fields of Asphodel, and my favorite, Tartarus, where powerful people's souls go. That is the deepest part of the universe. We sent the Titans there after the ten-year battle with the Olympians. Now, some are escaping and are planning to do battle once again with the Olympians. So, we who are elected will pronounce your punishment. Much as I would like to send you to Tartarus for your misdeeds, that place is in a chaotic state these days."

Suddenly, the youth in the chair stood up and pointed a finger at the trio. Without hesitation, words came pouring forth: "Wait a minute. I'm just a youngster. I don't know much about my soul yet. You can't pass judgment on such a young soul."

"Oh, but we can test your young soul."

"Like we said, we are offering this new service here in Hades," Minos spoke for the trio.

"So, what is this test all about? Eternal damnation? I attend a church, say my prayers, stay out of trouble, help around the house—"

He was cut off: "So you are young. We want to know your beliefs. What path are you taking?"

The boy continued: "I'm here on my own accord. I chose a pathway back where it divided into two. I let my friends go in one direction. I came along in another and ended up here now, before some committee to decide my fate. But I say, what fate? I haven't lived my life yet. Why all this talk about my soul?"

Aeacus spoke up, "Say, for a young lad, you've got a lot of spunk. What say we make up our minds as to what to do with this boy? I see the line is long today. Plenty of decisions to be made with those bad and evil souls comin' in here."

Rhadamanathus, the quiet judge, spoke up and summarized this occasion. "Son, if I may call you son, we all know what you and your new family are up to. You see, we report to Hades, and he already knows who you are, where you came from, and what you're up to. You have a mission ahead that will test every fiber of your being. Not just physical strength, but pure will of mind. Zeus, too, has been following your movements. As you know, he is doing battle with the Titans as we speak.

Oh, we can lock you up for a time. Starve you. Punish you physically. Torture your brain. We have our ways, and there would be no escape. As you say, damnation. Yes, damnation forever. But as to the verdict, my fine specimen of a deepening soul, go and do your battle thing. Use your wits. Take your feeble family friends with you. You have three choices when you reach your destination. You will be overwhelmed, and you will run scared away from all the tumult and chaos. You will sit on the sidelines and watch the two enemies probably destroy each other. Or you will choose to somehow serve as a go-between and try as you might, find some solution—partial or complete—to this fighting."

Minos continued: "Oh, that this life, or your life, were so simple . . . good versus evil, the right decisions, the wrong decisions, this road or that road, to laugh or to cry, to be jealous or to be kind, to be greedy or to be charitable, to be two-faced or to be honest . . . and on and on." Minos sighed and was breathless.

Rhadamanthus interrupted: "Minos, this new service we are offering mere mortals cannot be explained by your babbling of good, evil, on and on.

"We are to just remind clients—er—poor undeveloped souls, they have choices. Kind of like filling up an empty vessel. You know . . . good choice, bad choice, not-so-good choice, not-so-bad choice . . . on and on until the soul fills up, the mortal dies. We get 'em here. Pass judgment then. Case closed. Next victim—er—client. Er filled up soul. Repeat. Repeat. Repeat."

Aeacus spoke up: "We've spent too much time with this empty soul. He's got his skin, bone, and mindset to fill up his soul in the coming years. Then, upon his deathbed, he will return here front and center—or so we hope to be the case—to face our ultimate judgment. I say we cut him a deal. Just for the sake of decision-making, let's let him choose the river to cross back to where he came from. What say, young un? Pick one. Speak up. Please stand and address us."

The young boy hesitated, choosing his words carefully and proceeding to put one thought together after another in a formal yet compassionate way.

"I chose a path, one of two, many miles back. It, of course, led to this place. You say this is just a preview of what might come when I die, my soul filled. I don't know yet how I will lead my life. There are so many choices to make . . . decisions, some right, some wrong. I will give you some thanks for this preview. As to the river, I choose Phlegethon, the river of fire. I also hope my current family is safe and will be waiting for me at the battle site."

Minos reacted: "Good choice, my boy. But we have one last area of our underworld to show you."

Two soldiers quickly advanced, grabbing Bob's arms and marching him off to a waiting cart.

"As you are transported back to the river, you will pass by those lost souls whose fate has not yet been decided. Do they, one and all, deserve eternal torment with no room for redemption? Or can some earn their way to some form of respectability? Perhaps sending those souls up from these damnable depths? We're in constant consultation with the man himself—Hades. Personally, I find it difficult to pass judgment on most of these lost, wandering souls. The three of us are waiting for some formal pronouncement soon. Oh, by the way, you realize Rhea, by her very nature, is very protective of her brood. She birthed both Hades and Zeus. Be careful, young one. She may want them to be calmer and more peaceful in their respective domains, but she will nurture them, many at any cost. So good luck . . . ."

He was abruptly escorted to a cart pulled by a bear named Arktos. This bear belonged to Artemis but was being loaned to Hades as it has a bloodthirsty disposition.

The young boy shivered but trusted he would be safe. He was taken along a route leading to the river Phlegethon.

The rancid smell of rotting flesh was everywhere. Those bodies, which were mere skeletons, were cracked and split apart with pieces lying everywhere. Some partial organs were dried up and withering. The heat and stench in this part of the underworld was intolerable.

But where were the souls? This young boy was puzzled. Apparently, bodies came here still flesh-like and proceeded to rot.

No judgment as to where their souls would end up, as there were no souls to pass judgment on.

He could understand the questions those three individuals might have. How does one pass judgment on a non-entity?

Could these former selves, who now had little if any soul, be instructed somehow back to a wholeness of sorts, filling in missing pieces and assigned a soul of sorts?

It was too much to think about. Suddenly, Anktos reached back, grabbed the youth, and dumped him in a boat. The boy lay on his back, partially conscious, waiting to be ferried across the river. When he felt a hot, breathy wind blowing in his face, he slowly opened his eyes only to find another pair of eyes staring back at him. The craggy features of a skull brushed against the boy's face.

"You came to me earlier. I transported you across the river Styx. Now I find you are a young soul, not deep but shallow, innocent, naïve, not lost yet. I only transport lost souls. This system here is becoming more shaky every eon. New systems. Overburdened bureaucracy, I say. Still the Big Man in charge. Hopefully, he can make our lives here right again. Just a warning. You have been a visitor here. This is still the Underworld. So go lead your frantic, futile life above. Perhaps we will meet again. Hopefully, when all our haphazard ways are cleared up and we get back to some sense of normalcy, I say. So you don't need to be ferried back. The drifting current will take you to the other side. There you will be on your own. Meet up with your "family" somewhere near the Great Battlefield. So fill up your soul with your lifetime of experiences. May the gods, however you interpret them, be with you."

The young one was pushed onto the river and drifted across with the currents and gentle breezes, landing on an embankment on the other side.

9

The youth gathered himself and stood upright. In front of him were several passageways, and he was faced with choices once again.

His head was clearing, but the throbbing headaches continued. Where he had just been was now a fuzzy memory. He did remember his name. Bob. He was on some mission. Yes, forging ahead to some battlefield. His family, those creatures, and J.J., a friend whom he supposed was the leader who started this quest. A good term, he thought—*quest*.

He watched the sun set. He turned to the north and headed up the side of another craggy hill, the trail though straight and narrow, when he heard a cry from above. Someone or something was in pain, he thought. Swooping in a downward flight, fast, then faster, a creature landed on his shoulder. A large bird. An owl.

"Glaukes—what? Where did you come from? Oh joy, I'm meeting up with our family. Just ahead, yes?"

But the owl slumped on his shoulder, its wings now folded and eyes drooping. Where's J.J. and the rest of our group? Just ahead?" he repeated.

The owl snapped its head, seeming to say no.

"I never learned to read your body language. But then, where is our group? Are you giving me a message of false hope? Did something happen to all of them? Was their path worse than mine? Oh how I wish I could understand you. Should I follow you if you could lead me?" He knew he was going in the right direction toward Thessaly, which would take him to Mt. Othrys, the possible site of the great battle. His five senses were keen. He was aware of his surroundings. Glaukes remained calm on his shoulder.

Another sense arose in his mindset. Somehow, he knew he was being watched. He remembered something that was said about being protected by the Titan goddesses. What it meant, he could only guess. He also knew the angels were a part of this quest. Was it J.J. who told him that an archangel was part of this journey?

Anyway, he sensed now a higher order of angels present, maybe covering his every step. Which angel would step forward? Perhaps more than one to guide him into this battle?

Still, he sensed he had to take sides. The headaches were pounding him. He was tired and hungry, so he rested along this mountain trail. Glaukes slept on his shoulder.

As he lay on a flat, mossy bed, he felt his coat of many colors give off a glow he had not previously felt. The reds were throwing beams of light skyward. Again, didn't J.J. say this was the color of life and death—a coming of age? The rest of the colors lit up the sky. Barren darkness brought out the constellations this evening. He knew the North Star was positioned in its proper place this time of year.

He would continue his trek in the morning in that northern direction. His sleep was interrupted by a rustling sound. Before him lay a blanket with food items—meats, nuts, olives, and even seeds for Glaukes. They both had their fill that evening, and a comforting sleep came upon him. No questions were asked.

He was nearing his destination. He did have one brief dream. The name Mnemosyne streaked across his brain. It was clear now. He was putting past experiences together with what was happening now. Perhaps the Titan goddesses were finding a way to help him with this journey.

Morning came with a piercing ray of sunlight entering each eye. Quickly, he rose.

"Good morning, my friend." Glaukes flapped his wings. He seemed to be in good spirits, or so Bob thought. "Let's be off then. Catch the morning sun before the real heat sets in." Glaukes seemed to nod and turn his head more than ninety degrees.

A cool breeze blew across a large valley filled with olive and fig trees. The two creatures dined on olives and figs enough to last for a few hours.

"We must be coming to some form of civilization." Again, Glaukes seemed to be nodding while perched on Bob's shoulder.

If only I had been taught a lesson on how to understand this owl, I might be able to communicate back and forth. Suddenly, Glaukes flapped his wings and began screeching, a wild, frantic cry.

"What is it? Danger ahead?"

From behind a row of fig trees, two objects charged at the two figures. Bob thought quickly and took out a slinger from the case he was carrying. It normalized in size. He started to load it with a rock he found, but it was too late. The two creatures knocked him to the ground. The box of weapons flew open, releasing the contents—all the weapons he was given to protect himself.

The mauling began—or rather the licking. First, his leg was licked. Then his arms. Finally, a smack on the cheeks. As he sat up, the two creatures came close to Bob's face and nuzzled against his neck, one on each side.

"Boys! It's you! K'yon 1 and K'yon 2!"

Glaukes' flapping stopped. He rested again on Bob's shoulder, and the two creatures were content to rest on each side of him. They weren't growling now but instead were making a purring sound, a soft, quiet tone.

Bob, always at a loss for telling them apart, wished again that J.J. would have clued him in and taught him the subtle differences. Each creature in the kingdom he knew was unique, but why hadn't he learned the differences between these two dogs?

But why? Where is J.J.? Is she alive? Bob knew the battlefield was near. As he rose, one of the dogs nudged him from behind.

"You want us to follow you? Where are we going?"

His thoughts were muddled. He was aware that only J.J. knew how to communicate with these animals. As the dogs jumped and barked for attention, he sensed what that meant. They want him to follow.

"Ah, one of you has a higher-pitched sound than the other. But then, is that K'yon 1 or K'yon 2? The dogs seemed to become annoyed at Bob's facial expressions. His face was confused, hesitant, afraid, and even expressionless.

"Okay, boys, take us where J.J. is located." His last sensation before being led was that of a strange odor in the air. He couldn't figure it out at first. Then it hit him. The putrid smell from the depths of Hades, of rotting flesh. Now he knew the battlefield was ahead, ever so near.

The dogs bounced along in the valley, and the two other travelers did likewise with Glaukes on Bob's shoulder and the dogs leading the way.

10

The rumblings grew loud; then, there was an explosion, which set off lightning strikes across the darkened sky. The meadow just ahead of the group burst into flames. The dogs went wild. Their barking echoed across the valleyed meadow. Glaukes retreated, his wings drooping and eyes shut.

Bob stopped in his tracks when a blow landed squarely behind his right ear.

It laid him prone. Then a sharp object stabbed at his heels. He lunged ahead and turned to see an armored body above him. There was no time to open the case he was carrying with all the implements of war inside. Rolling away from this figure, he rose and was behind him.

The warrior lunged at his victim. Bob sidestepped his advance. He suddenly shouted, "Attack, attack!" The dogs pounced on the intruder. Parts of his body were unprotected, and they tore at this flesh. The soldier dropped his weapon. Blood gushed from the wounds. Soon, he was mostly silent.

His final words: "Zeus rules. Humans die." This hoplite must have been a forward observer who saw this group advancing and tried to take them out.

In a flash, the red coloring on his coat lit up the sky. He felt a chill. His own flesh crawled with goosebumps. The dogs heeled over the dead body. Glaukes opened his eyes, let out a peep, then relaxed on Bob's shoulder.

A wisp of cool air brushed by his face. He reached up to quell the tickling but stopped. A message seemed to enter his brain. What was it? *A seraphim is with you now.*

He wished somewhere along the passageway he would have discussed the hierarchy of angels with J.J. At least he knew some of the goddesses were helping his family, and now the angels. But he was still threatened with those words: "Zeus rules. Humans die."

It seemed strange to him that all was calm again. The meadow was charred and destroyed. No more lightning lit up the sky.

There must be some village or civilization up ahead. The group again banded together and moved across the burned-out meadow.

On the other side, a wider path lay ahead. Where they would meet up with J.J. and Rhea, he could only guess. He assumed they were still alive.

Then he remembered Mt. Othrys was near a town in Thessaly. Almost by instinct, his movements were going in the direction of this town. He also felt responsible for the fate of his animal friends. Finding a shelter against a prominent mountain escarpment, the crew bedded down for the night.

Orion, Scorpius, Cygnus, and Cassiopeia were all visible this evening. Other constellations, too, bore tribute to the Greek gods who were honored by the wise citizens of Greece many eons ago.

Bob awoke as he was lightly brushed by some force moving gently across his face. A blanket was laid down on a stone pathway. Many varieties of fruits, cheeses, and olives covered the surface.

Strips of lamb and bacon were in a pot.

K'yon 1 and 2 were the first to notice the food and scampered to the lamb first.

"Not so fast, my friends. Wait until Glaukes and I are seated." The dogs drooled and growled, but obeyed his command.

Glaukes surveyed the spread and seemed to frown, then perched on Bob's shoulder.

"Ah, there may not be much for you here. No bugs or little creatures to devour." He smiled, his mild manner still concerned for where Glaukes would find his source of food.

"Out there. The meadow is your answer." Glaukes flew off. Though burned and charred, the meadow contained many of life's little creatures sufficient to supply Glaukes with a full meal.

The dogs and Bob ate in peace. The journey today would probably lead them to Mt. Othrys. Zeus would be watching his every move.

He felt a strong need to be around J.J. and Rhea, but advice from them was only a direction to follow or a decision to make about this war business. He hadn't used his weapons yet. He sensed strange forces were moving him forward, but he felt comfortable at this time and place.

11

Moving northeast, they came upon a river where they chose to rest and find a snack among the many groves of olive and fig trees. The dogs could bathe in the river to cool off.

"How are we doing?" Bob thought now he could read the owl's thoughts. He detected some nervous flapping of wings. The owl, peering toward the northeast, squawked a bit.

"We'll get there by nightfall. Then, we'll find a place to stay the night. There must be humans we can talk to and find out what is going on." His mind is now very clear. "This river's name is Peneus. If we follow it, we'll reach Thessaly by nightfall. Forward ho, gang!"

There is a renewed spirit of joy with the group. The dogs, tails wagging, ears perking, skipped along the river's trail. Glaukes, however, eyes alert, head moving side to side, cautiously sensed his surroundings.

Leaves on the trees rustled, fluttering in step with the group. They stopped. The movement of the leaves stopped. There would be a bend up ahead, a clearing. They reached this point. Ahead over another clearing, the town of Thessaly.

They heard a loud cry from behind a tree. Then another. Then another. A sword aimed at Bob. The dogs were pounced on and muzzled.

Strange words came from one of the men who was clothed in battle gear. Now, several of these men made an appearance.

The soldier who was their leader came face-to-face with Bob. He uttered the word "desmates" then ordered his men to tie Bob up and march him along. The dogs were carried in a cage.

This soldier spoke another term, which, for some reason, Bob could understand—"Phylakimemos." He knew he was identified as an enemy and was being brought somewhere to be placed under armed guards. He was a captive, a prisoner of these warriors.

During this skirmish, Glaukes flew away to parts unknown.

They were taken to a large marble building, ornate in structure, yet a chill in the air presupposed this place to be a place of terror and brutality.

The cell was dark. No light penetrated between the bars. His head ached and pounded. He blacked out and awoke to the rattling of keys and stomping feet.

"Arise. To the Hall of Justice. Your fate is in their hands." Two armed guards jerked him out of his cell, down a hallway, up some stairs, down another hallway, and finally into a large room filled with statues of Greek gods and goddesses. Large ionic pillars held up the ceiling.

"Hold his head up. I want to see his full face." A guard swiftly lifted Bob's chin. He was face-to-face with a large male dressed in a toga, wearing sandals. The male paced back and forth. Then, he stopped.

"Your name, young man—Atlas? Apollo? Adonis? Achilles?"

"No, the name is Bob," he stated firmly.

"Bob, is it. What a simple, mundane, boring one. No tribute to the gods with such a mindless name."

"Where are the dogs? I demand to know where they are. Are they safe?"

"Oh, you demand, do you?" A guard again lifted his chin, this time snapping it a bit.

"Do you know who we are? Do you know where you are? Let me fill you in, Bob."

Bob thought it unusual he could understand what this soldier was saying. Still, J.J. said wearing the coat would help to translate languages. He didn't bother to ask how that worked, which was another of his missed opportunities to learn more about the intricate details of this mission.

"We are the Myrmidons, a warrior tribe whose job it is to protect Zeus. Now you enter our land, a strange group of beings zigzagging into our presence. You know, Zeus has been following your merry band of interlopers. For some reason, he feels threatened as his own mother has been accompanying you on your journey."

Bob broke in: "So, where are Rhea and my other friend?"

"Your other friend?" This warrior came close to Bob's face. "We have heard of a busybody interfering with our history, sticking a nose in our history . . . something about a portal.

"My boss is the ultimate warrior. We will protect his ultimate number one position in the cosmos. Right now, he is recapturing the Titans who escaped from Tartarus. Our gods who fight among themselves are their business and not yours or any other human form.

I often regret the time the first man, Phaenon, was formed from clay and water. You humans have done nothing to distinguish yourself as a species. I believe all of you are at the bottom of the chain of life. The gods give you fire, and you use it to burn down your forests. The gods provide you with water, and you destroy your oceans and lakes, polluting them with your garbage. The gods give you the ability to raise crops as a chief food source, and you waste most of it. And why is a large segment of your population food-insecure and starving? Our gods, at one time, were harmonious and taught you how to become a family. Still, you continue with your anger and animosity. Men and women don't understand each other and continue to destroy each other.

"So, you come here with your boyish ways—ignorant, naïve, still dependent on your parents for financial support and instructions as to how to grow up to become mature and an independent thinking adult. Why here in this land, our teens are adults. I ask, why does it take so long in your world through that portal?

"We have our warriors out looking for that J.J. of yours. When we find her, we will negate any power she possesses and will destroy the secret she may have with all that portal business.

"As for you, we will test your will and find out your weaknesses. We'll exploit them, yet make you into a warrior. Maybe you can become one of our low-level guards, worshipping Zeus, and live to carry out his every wish.

"And as for Rhea, her loyalties lie with her children, not a foreign invader like yourself.

"Tomorrow you will begin the challenge. Then I will introduce you to my crew, who individually will challenge your strength and resolve."

Bob was led back to his cell. A large meal was prepared and given to him to eat. The next day, he would be tested in a life-and-death struggle for his survival.

He wondered where J.J. was and if Rhea was really more concerned with her own children. And where had Glaukes disappeared to? And whether the dogs were safe. His mood went from fear to concern to anger that he had allowed himself to get to this point. He didn't seem to have the ability to figure out what was happening to him. And he was thinking of finding J.J., getting to a portal, and being transported home, which now seemed hard to imagine ever returning to.

Lights went out in this sub-basement. It was dark, dank, and dirty, but the day had come to an end, and sleep was a welcome relief.

12

Once again, the sound of clinking keys and stomping boots woke him up. The guards escorted him to a building that housed much exercise equipment. Ropes hung from the ceiling. Pads were on the floor. Athletes exercised throughout this facility.

"Bring him over here." The chief warrior instructed Bob to sit and listen to his directions. "No talking. Sorry, no breakfast this morning. Only water here when you need it. You will be in two events: one for strength and one for speed. Let me introduce you to your competitors. Kratos, over here. You see these weights. Whoever lifts the most is the winner. We will keep adding weights onto this bar. Whoever loses strength first and can lift no more loses.

"The second event is speed. Over here, Nike. She will race you five laps around our gym. Simple again. One runner will be ahead of the other runner at the end of the race.

"You, Bob, must win both events to help yourself with your release. You lose one or both events, and Zeus will decide your fate. You may win one and have a lighter sentence depending on the decision Zeus makes."

Kratos approached the weights. His large, muscled frame stood in direct contrast to Bob's somewhat spindly arms, thin pipes for legs, and slender back.

Kratos, the first to lift, hoisted a hundred pounds of weights (marble shaped like a pipe) over his head. He dropped it gently to the ground.

Bob, next up, felt the wrath of Kratos, who was staring at this thin, somewhat weak human. He stood over the weight, looked up at the ceiling, then bowed down and started to lift. He felt his muscles snap and twitch as he grunted with agony. The pipe went overhead. He dropped it, slamming it to the ground.

"Add some weights," a judge announced. Kratos again lifted the added weights with ease and gently placed them on the ground. Even so, he was working up a sweat, and it started to dribble off his massive beard. He snarled at Bob, wanting just to end this nonsense.

Bob took this extra weight and began his lift. He winced and grimaced as he again lifted the pipe over his head. Again, it came down with a loud thud. His shoulders ached, and he was out of breath. *Perhaps*, he thought, *the conditioning he labored through during the football season was beginning to pay off.*

Now, Kratos, his face crimson, was livid and losing his patience. Add more weights. When approaching the weights this time, he bumped Bob chest to chest.

"*Afti ti for a chaneis.*" Bob knew what this meant: "This time you lose." With much heavier weights on each end of the pipe, he lifted it, straining, face contorted, until it rose above his head. He roared as the weight dropped. "*Itta; itta!*" (victory), which did mean I won—my victory.

Bob approached the weights for the third time. He made a worthwhile attempt to lift the weights but became exhausted with the effort. "Yes, Kratos, *itta*."

He extended his right hand in thanks and respect. Kratos

grabbed his forearm and held it for a moment. Words were not spoken. They separated.

One of the judges quickly appeared in front of Bob. He cried out: "*Apollymi*," meaning, you lost the competition.

He ushered him to a track and placed him at the starting line. Help up three fingers and motioned around the arena. Suddenly, a winged figure stood by him, her white dress flowing. She wore a gold and green tiara and golden sandals.

"This is Nike, goddess of victory," another judge announced. "So, three times around the arena. Straight race. Winner takes all."

Bob wondered what that meant. So, he was racing a lady with wings who could obviously fly? Speed was her game. Unfair.

Just as another negative thought entered his mind, he heard, "Racers, I will position the hysplex across the starting line. One card will be placed at waist level, the other at knee level. When the signal is given, I will drop the cord; you will then start to run."

The signal to start flashed. The cord dropped. Nike was off in a flash, Bob plodding behind.

Three laps concluded. The crowd that had gathered to watch shouted out, "Record time, Nike! Poor fellow was eating your dust."

Bob was told to finish the three laps. Puffing home across the finish line, he sensed he had lost more than just a race.

Nike sped away in a hurry. Bob's arms were pinned back, and he was ushered to the corner of the gym. The leader of the Myrmidons came over to address him.

"You have lost both events. We only tested you in two events.

You see those two over there?" He pointed at two figures standing against a far wall. "That one is Bia, goddess of force. And that one is Zelos, god of rivalry. You see, all four are demigods who carry out and protect Zeus' interests. They do what he tells them. Life and death in most cases. And you have failed our tests.

"You will be jailed in our tower to await your fate. You may have a few minutes to plead your case to spare your life, but I wouldn't count on it," he said, his voice trailing off. Yawning, he summoned the guards to take him away.

Bob, startled and angry, felt every emotion coming to a boil. "This is absurd nonsense. What kind of chance did I have? What place is this anyway? So, I know I am close to Zeus. You say he will make a decision about the fate of my life. What does he care about one tiny human being? Isn't he busy fighting the Titans again? Many have escaped from Tartarus, haven't they? So much bloodshed. So much fighting. You know what? If he is making a decision on my fate, he must be frightened of me. Or at least concerned enough to give me some respect. After all, I made this trip with his mother, Rhea, and J.J.— "

The chief warrior broke in. "There's that name again. That woman who knew the process, finding the portal. She brought those animals with her and convinced Rhea that there is hope to address our concerns. Where is she? We've lost her whereabouts."

He approached Bob and poked him in the chest. "Tell me, you pathetic excuse for a flesh and blood being, where is she?"

Bob stood still. He had said too much already.

"Take him to the tower."

This night left him with an unbearable headache, an empty

stomach, and many questions he could not answer. He pinched himself. *Ouch*. Not a dream. Then what? *I need J.J. to find the portal here so I can get back home*. But then that existence was no more pleasant or satisfying than this dimension, far out in some past cosmos.

He was greeted in his tower cell with crickets chirping, fireflies lighting up the outside night air, an occasional sad cry of a wolf, and spiders busy spinning their webs, capturing their prey—mosquitoes, flies, gnats, and flying bugs that unceremoniously flew into the webbed net. *Fate*, he thought. *More than just decision-making*. And he fell asleep on a hard board with a frog croaking his own woes away.

He heard a light tapping on the bar of the window. Then another tapping, more pronounced. Bob lifted himself from a shallow slumber and came face to face with the owl. "Glaukes, it's you, in the flesh. Oh, I want to hug you, stroke your feathers. You're here. You found me! But how? Where did you come from? J.J.? Is she alive? Where is she?"

The owl lifted its head and turned it forty-five degrees. He shut one eye, then hooted. Bob knew enough now that he understood what Glaukes was telling him.

"Get back to J.J. Bring her here. But tell her to be careful. Her life's at stake. These warriors are going to decide my fate tomorrow. She must figure out a plan to get me out of here. I have to find a portal and get back to my real home—with my original family. My own fate is in your hands, Glaukes. You have a job to do—isn't that what J.J. said? Or was it Rhea? And can Rhea be trusted? I love you, Glaukes . . . my second family friend."

The owl fluttered away. Bob hoped he understood his instructions. He slumped back on the wooden bed. The lights were still out, and the crickets kept on chirping.

A breakfast of lamb, olives, figs, and a mush the guard called cereal was placed on the floor of the cell. "Last meal, eh, young fella. Saw ya losin' those contests. Our boys here are men your age. No time for playin' and foolin' around. Sorry, chum—you seem like a nice enough kid, but me thinks the devil wants your unfulfilled soul. Sorry, I got to put the hood on ya and the cuffs. Come on along, sonny. Say bye-bye to this here Imperial Palace. Nice accommodations, eh?"

Bob was learning this language quickly. While he was maturing mentally, becoming smarter, he sensed a lot of knowledge was not what it was cracked up to be. Decision-making and choices seemed far more important.

A tall, elegant man, clothed in a toga and wearing sandals, walked back and forth in front of Bob, occasionally stopping to peer into his eyes.

"An unusual case. Certainly different. No clear evidence— right or wrong. Not up to Greek standards, physically, maybe even mentally. Thought process not fully developed.

"A stray. A youth meandering, wandering, crossing into our territory. An interloper to be sure. But just a young lad with two dogs in tow who wants to see the big battle. That such a wee lad would want to do such a thing. What, for a thrill? This is dangerous territory, my boy. My thought is that someone put you up to this venture of yours. There's someone else out there, a J.J. something. Smart, savvy, a woman who knows the portal system, who knows our ways, the ways of the gods. And to have Rhea help, no less. My, my—a different sort of case no less.

"Oh no, Bob. I'm just the one pronouncing the decision. We're waiting here in the great hall for the big man's decision. Yes, the case just kept going up the line all the way to him, Zeus. Can you believe that? The supreme ruler has all the decisions to make day to day, and he's deliberating on your fate as we speak.

"Maybe Mom had something to do with his decision, or maybe it was the most supreme influencer of the cosmos, Gaia, Rhea's mother."

Polished bronze doors led into a large dome-shaped room. The ceiling consisted of moving mosaics of a cloudy sky and thunderbolts. The side walls flashed lightning bolts. On a large throne chair meant for royalty sat the ultimate Olympian. His demeanor demanded respect. His face contorted, taking in the many sorrows and woes that plagued him and the other Olympians.

On each side sat his council members—Kratus, Bia, Zelos, and Nike. They were tense and warlike, ready to protect their boss.

The woman approached the throne.

"Halt," ordered Bia, motioning for the woman to step on a platform. "No closer. State who you are—your case. I will translate. He will give you an answer. Then you will depart; two Hoplite guards will escort you out."

"Thank you for allowing me this brief time to plead a case

that has come to my attention. A most urgent case.

"I am Themus, a Titan goddess. Of course, you, the Great One, know me as representative for divine law throughout the cosmos.

"This urgent matter is that of a young boy named Bob. He and others with him have come here through the portal system. His group is on a quest to end up here to intercede in some way and to help quell the tensions, animosity, and hatred that exist between the Titans and Olympians. Now, you have captured him, held him hostage, and are going to pass judgment on the fate of his young soul.

"Yes, our cosmos is in a state of chaos. What a band of humans and animals can do to help our plight may be open to conjecture. But let me explain further. This boy has remained chaste in his pursuits. He has not lifted any weapons, vanquishing any supposed enemy.

"By Greek law, custom, and tradition, he has met the standards set for the variety of ways to express love. Eight ways in fact.

"He has been challenged along the way, confronting dangers from our gods and others. He and his family have succeeded in caring for these concerns, performing a caretaking role of the highest magnitude.

"Briefly, Bob spent time with Hades. Their decision was to send him on his way with a warning to fill his soul over his lifetime with kind deeds, dutiful service to others, and to remain loyal to the many families he may encounter throughout his human existence.

"Now, I find he and his family have been followed by the

highest order of angels, a seraphim, a most zealous angel. One next to God.

"I know you, the Great One, have tracked his and his family's every move. You know his story. His intentions are just and honorable.

"What say you? My request as the supreme representative for divine law in the universe is to set him free and help him find the portal for his return to his own human kingdom."

Bia interrupted: "Stop. You have stated the case. No more shedding of your tears. I will confer. His answer is final. No turning back."

The five figures huddled, whispering to one another. The largest figure snarled, and a lightning bolt bounced off all four walls. The sky from the dome grew dark. No stars were lit. All was quiet. A verdict was rendered. Bia stood close to Themus.

"He has come to his conclusion. Bob will be free from sun up to sun up. He will not be followed. If he can find the portal, so be it. If not, we will recapture him and make him a low-level hoplite to remain here and be subject to the laws of the Underworld. His flesh will rot, and his bones will decay. A soul only worthy of Hades' calling will be left. Then eternal damnation. Our guards will release him, and he will maintain his freedom for two sun-ups. Now go and do your bidding elsewhere. Your divine laws are a misfit for our purposes. Guards, escort Themus away."

Again, lightning flashed. This episode echoed throughout the cosmos. Thunderbolts, too, boomed a warning to the Great One's enemies. He still rules. Titans will be rounded up and returned to their underworld prison.

Themus was gone. It was left to the Greek wearing the toga

and sporting fancy sandals to explain Bob's fate.

"You will have one last meal. We are cordial that way, you know. Then it will be goodbye for two sun-ups. Tomorrow morning, you will make haste, I'm sure to stay alive for one more day."

He spent the night, again, in the tower cell. Sunup would come none too soon.

13

The bronze door in the back of the compound opened. He was left in an alleyway, alone, wondering which direction to go.

By a dumpster was an open bag of sunflower seeds. He stuffed his pockets until they bulged. He would drop these seeds, and if he came upon them again, he would know he would be returning his steps. There must be some logic to his decision-making, he thought. There were seven figures in his family.

He didn't know if K'yon 1 and 2 would be released. Probably not. Or could they possibly escape their captors? They were very smart and well-trained by J.J., so it was a distinct possibility, he thought.

Glaukes could be anywhere, making contact with J.J. if she is still alive. Again, the owl well-trained by J.J.

As to Rhea, it was anyone's guess. She could have me followed if she were working for Zeus. After all, she is his mother, and a mother's love is unbounded. So, he told himself to descend Mt. Olympus into the valley below. There were small hamlets he would find. Perhaps find a church. Yes, he would talk to a minister, a priest, someone of the clergy. They would hide him, protect him for a while.

The rocky descent meant trekking over rough terrain step by step. Somewhere at the bottom, he would find sanctuary. He left this thought as down a stone-encrusted trail to a small hamlet he was led.

Then appeared a small town square with a park in the middle. At one end was a church of marble, old but in a Greek classic style. His heart pounded as he surmised part of a journey's end. Approaching carefully, he climbed the front steps and pulled on the latch to the enormous wooden double door—it was locked.

He banged on it several times. No response. He got the same result after going around to the back. He tried peering in through a stained-glass window, but it was too foggy to see clearly inside.

Sitting on some side steps, he contemplated his next move. He found some berries and figs to eat in a grove next to the church. The next morning, sunup would begin the hunt for him if not already. Then a major thought hit him. What if he made the trek to Athens to the Parthenon? Perhaps those real ancient Greek philosophers could help him. He thought Athens to be some sort of sanctuary city filled with people who believed in democratic principles, free speech, the freedom to express one's views unabated by autocratic rules and regulations.

He gave himself over to a few hours of sleep here in this grave, then it would be up and onward. In his mind, he converted the distance to miles and calculated two hundred and forty. A lofty goal to be motivated to go there. He calculated the direction. Hopefully, a straight and narrow pathway.

The sun glared in his eyes. Without an alarm clock, he had overslept. A rooster filled the village with wake-up calls. It was time to get to business. People already scurried about, and the marketplace was filling up with vendors and customers.

Moving quickly, he moved to the edge of town. The early morning sun directed him to move in that easterly direction.

The time passed quickly. He passed one village, then another, then fell along a straight pathway with the sun now behind him. To his surprise, no soldiers were blocking his way! He met nobody on this trail. His next job was to find a food source. His body ached; his feet hurt, having been stung by a patch of nettles he walked into; and his stomach growled, *feed me, feed me*.

If he could keep this pace up, and there was no one about to arrest or rob him, then he could reach Athens in a week or so.

Evening seemed to come quickly. A small lake appeared in a forested area just off this part of the pathway. Sitting on a bank, he peered into the clear, cold water. Sticking his feet in the water invited small fish to nibble at his toes. What if I can take a branch, whittle it somehow into a spear, and catch some of these nibblers?

His suitcase of military equipment was taken by Zeus' guards at the time he was captured. "Now I could use those weapons to sustain my life," he told himself. The first attempt proved futile. Then one swam right on the stick as he thrust it into the water. Then another hooked on.

Building a fire would almost prove as futile as catching a fish. Rubbing then pounding two rocks together didn't produce a spark to the leaves and twigs he piled up in his self-designed fire pit. Then it happened. A large spark ignited the pile. He quickly stoked it with limbs and branches he found lying around the pit.

He had gutted the two fish before igniting the fire. They lay on a hard board, which he knew would burn. But he timed it just right so that the fish were cooked and the board was only slightly burnt.

From the shoreline of the lake, he pulled three cattails from the water, knowing the ends were edible, rather sweet, and delicious.

The fire died out. He took a swim and prepared to bed down for the night. He hustled to build a small fort out of branches and moss plastered onto the crisscrossed design.

Sleep came quickly. The sky lit up with constellations he was familiar with. He thought it strange as tinted colors seemed to streak across the sky this evening—red, blue, purple, and white— the same shades on his jacket he still wore.

A glowing light, a firefly perhaps, came nearer and nearer to his face this evening. Then it passed swiftly by and was gone. For an instant, he was in a dream state and could think of nothing else but an angel, a seraphim.

He slept soundly and awoke to the croaking of frogs. Again, the sun pierced his eyes, reminding him that his head continued to throb. The headaches worsened, becoming more intense than ever.

The next morning, he scoured the area around the small lake and found berries and again cattails. He sensed that at some point along the way, he would need some form of meat to help him sustain his endurance. Perhaps he would find a farmhouse, a place here in the country where a family kept animals, chickens, sheep, lambs. But could he take the chance on exposing himself to the scrutiny of whomever he came upon?

He would be careful, but as the trip progressed, he got weaker. While his will was still strong, his energy level waned.

The noon sun blazed on his entire body; his arms, legs, and head were burnt by Helios. He sought shade in which to rest for an hour or so. His sense of timing was acute. Just one hour, then back on the trail again.

A shack in the near distance shimmered from the rays. Relief to come. This was some type of shelter; maybe a hunter built it as a blind refuge waiting to shoot at some prey. In any case, it was large enough inside to lie prone on the floor. Now, for sure, welcome relief.

Complete deep sleep overcame him. The air was still outside. Inside, too, no sound except for some deep breathing—in, out, in, out.

A hand clasped over his mouth, and liquid was poured down his throat. He gagged but didn't wake up. Then another few ounces of a substance. This time, he opened his eyes. He heard voices and tried to scream, but was silenced into submission.

14

"He's coming to." Voices filled the air. Hours later, he was in another place. Startled, he tried to sit up but was forced on his back again.

His eyes focused, then he shouted out in relief, panic, and fear, "J.J., it's you, really you." This time, he sat up, and no one forced him down. "But how? You're alive!"

J.J. interrupted: "One question at a time. One answer at a time."

"My heart is racing. All that time away from my family. Where are the others? What's going on?"

Suddenly, Glaukes landed on J.J.'s shoulder.

"Glaukes, it is you. You sweet, soulful creature." Tears rolled down Bob's cheeks. Coming out of a shadow above him, a form appeared. "Rhea, too, you're here. Our family. How are K'yon 1 and 2? Did they escape?"

"As I said, one question at a time." J.J. went on: "Sorry, we had to bring you here this way. You'll be okay in another hour or so. Eleusinian is the drug. It has a hallucinogenic side effect, but nothing serious. You see, we were all working together to keep track of you. The dogs escaped and tracked your scent. Glaukes came upon your scattered seeds and followed the trail. Rhea took care of her boy, Zeus, by stalling to keep him from sending out the troops to arrest you again, take you back, and make a low-ranking soldier out of you. A futile life story that would have been.

"And me, what did I do, you ask? I orchestrated your journey, but I let you have the freedom to choose your own path. I didn't interfere with your decision-making. For a while, I thought all was lost—that you would become just another lost soul forever to seek your true purpose in your human state. But you surprised us. You came through. All the colors on your coat are still intact. And the fact you didn't open your weapons box is an added bonus."

"Now, I'm totally confused. So, who are you really, J.J.? Where did you come from? Why was I chosen?"

"Odd questions. Already answered. Say no more. My job here is done. Oh, there are still problems with the gods, the Olympians, and the Titans. Maybe there always will be . . ."

Bob spoke up again: "So what, in fact, was our mission? If not to help the gods with their problems, then what?"

"You are growing in your wit and wisdom. You are flesh and blood. Your divine presence is needed on your planet. Use your newfound skills wisely. Begin your own quest on Earth to lead a soul-centered life, not an ego-centered life." J.J. smiled and caressed Bob's forehead.

"I know you have been puzzled from the start. But I now know your heart and soul will work together to live that soul-centered life."

Bob, still inquisitive, asked, "So, where are we? What is this place? How do I get back home?"

"Not so fast," said J.J., holding his arm. "That church you came to is our home base. This is where we enter and exit into the cosmos."

"That church where I am music director is also a special place, a place filled with the stories of gods and goddesses. But we know the practice of worshipping one God is now in what we call modern times.

We discovered a portal there many years ago, but just now are we beginning to make use of it."

Bob spoke up: "So more humans will be brought through that portal to experience what I have experienced?"

"Please—don't confuse what this is all about as an experience. It's much more—deeper rooted in the soul," said J.J., frowning slightly.

"Okay, begin reading—your human 'experience,' everything you can about the soul. You have your, as you say, authors who purport to put their feeble thoughts on paper in story or book form about the many aspects of the soul.

"Study these ideas. Create your own mindset. Continue to live your life as soulful as you are able. But enough for now. Time for us to part ways." She motioned for him to come face-to-face with a large door similar to the door he came through when he started his adventure.

Bob turned his head. He noticed J.J., her face serene, angelic. She seemed to be floating slightly, her feet off the ground.

"Can I say goodbye to my friends? My family? Where are they? Where is Rhea? Glaukes? The dogs? Even the lions?"

J.J. merely added, "Your journey is not ended. It's only just begun. You will meet many humans and animals in your brief lifetime on your planet. Treat them with respect. Love them—all of humanity. Remember, you achieved all of the Greeks' ways of loving. And, finally, you found self-love, the ability to glow exuberantly from within."

Bob put his hand on the door, wanting just one more question answered: "What then, J.J., do I call you?"

"Just call me The Lady in the Loft." With that expression, the door opened, inducing a flurry of activity. After a cloudy moment, Bob found himself sitting in the front row of his own church, looking straight up at the altar.

He wanted to go home. His own home. His stomach growled. He felt as if he hadn't eaten in a week.

His mother greeted him at the door. "So, where have you been these past twelve hours? Don't you know it's almost midnight? Where did you think you were going? You're not dating anyone. You can't drive. Where did you run off to this morning? Wait till your dad comes in. He's out in the barn repairing that old John Deere. You were supposed to help him today—learn what this farm is all about. You disappoint me, Bob."

"Are you going to listen to me, or not?" asked Bob, speaking up.

"Say, don't take that tone of voice with me, young man," his mother said, now approaching a state of rage.

"I was at church. Sorry, I didn't tell you. I met someone. Went on a trip . . ."

"What kind of trip?" she asked. "Did someone take you somewhere? You know you're not to go anywhere with strangers."

"No, no one took me anywhere. It all happened in the church. Or I think it did."

"What happened in the church?" his mother asked, looking concerned. "Is there a new group for bible study? Say, did you join the choir?"

"Well, maybe. And, no, I didn't join the choir."

"Well, what then? What do you mean, maybe? Maybe what? And who were you talking to?"

"It was the choir director, Ms. Janina, J.J. She just talked to me about my soul."

"Your soul. A mighty deep subject, wouldn't you say? And you spent these past twelve hours talking to her about your soul?" His mother was starting to look more worried.

"Well, not exactly. We went on an adventure. A trip. Out in the cosmos . . ."

"Hold it there, bud. What kind of trip? Were drugs involved? That woman hasn't been here that long. I've had my suspicions about her. Kind of an eccentric, I'd say."

"No, it wasn't like that at all. We just talked. She's a nice person. Not odd or anything. I've been doing some custodial work there—volunteering hours for my Eagle Scout program."

"So today you helped around the church? Is that it? No other crazy wild story?"

"Sort of. Well, yes." Bob was tiring of this line of questioning.

"I'll have a talk with this lady on Sunday after services. See what she's up to. Seems a simple request to ask you to join the choir or a bible study group is all she needs to do. Come out with it. Plain and simple."

"Can I go to my room now? I'm tired. It's been a long day."

"Okay, your dad will talk to you tomorrow. They'll be heck to pay. You know he's going to skin you alive. He needs you to help more around here. There's been talk our homestead is goin' belly up.

"Crops out in the field not producing again. Chickens aren't layin' as many eggs. Too many repairs on the place to count on your hands and feet. Even old Gramps and Grandma are talking about going to the old folks' home. They say it may be less expensive than hangin' around here takin' up room and board.

"Yes, I'll have a word with that woman, J.J.; you're being mighty casual with just initials. I'd say she wants something from you. Maybe to be her assistant or something. Overall, you are a responsible young man, I would say. Go to your room then and get a good night's sleep."

Lying in bed, he looked up at the constellations illuminated on the ceiling. He had memorized quite a few of them. He knew their movements around the universe and was especially familiar with those constellations the ancient Greeks designated as tributes to their gods.

As he lay awake, he felt his headache subside. There was a sense, too, of satisfaction in the way he felt about today's experience, or journey as J.J. preferred to call it.

But just twelve hours had elapsed by these earthly standards. He did feel different, but he wasn't sure why or if these feelings were permanent.

Yes, by all means, too, I'm going to talk to her Sunday after services, he thought. *I'll find out more about what went on today, or it seemed longer than that in my own thought process.*

This talk of a portal. Who would believe it? Better to keep this between me and J.J.. She surely would tell me more. Help me understand what I experienced. There's that word again. J.J. telling me no – then maybe a divine intervention.

My thoughts are muddled, but somehow I do feel the start of something. A trip. To where. For what purpose?

Yes, J.J. will help me clarify my thoughts. Sunday can't come too soon.

15

The service ended. Bob's mother told Bob she would be going up to the loft in a few minutes. She was meeting with some ladies first from the Ladies Auxiliary.

He ascended the steps, eager to talk to J.J. and ask some questions. Gain some more knowledge. This idea of a soul.

The lady's back was turned as Bob approached her. He knew J.J. to be jumpy, quirky in that way, so he waited for her to turn around.

She turned and, with a still demeanor, said, "Yes, can I help you, young man?"

"Janina Jerusalem?" Bob blurted out.

"Yes, I said, how can I help you?"

"But . . . but you're not the Janina Jerusalem I know."

"What are you talking about? I'm the music director here. Janina Jerusalem. Do you have a problem with that? Again, what do you want?"

"I, ah, nothing really. It's just that you don't look like the person I thought you'd be like. I'm confused."

"So, if you'll excuse me, I have these papers to collect and the organ to turn off. I have to meet with Father. Good day, young man." She excused herself and descended the stairs behind Bob.

It occurred to Bob that every time over this past month when he met with Janina, no one else was around. The head custodian was in the church but never talked to Janina nor came up to the loft.

Come to think of it, Janina met with Bob after she said choir practice was over, and everyone had left the church.

So, who was the Janina Jerusalem Bob had come to know—especially on their divine journey together? He still had questions to ask and few, if any, answers. So how would he explain all this to his parents and grandparents? They would say what a wild imagination he had . . . maybe such a fantasy life as to be completely detached from reality, perhaps a psychosis worthy of some form of psychiatric treatment.

Before descending the steps, he peered out to the hallway where he and Janina went through that door—a portal, she said. *So how do I explain that to anyone?*

A pecking on the stained-glass window got his attention, and he looked out. Looking back was an owl, screeching, wanting attention. "Glaukes, my friend. How are you? Thanks for all your help. We are family, aren't we?"

On his walk home this Sunday, he heard sudden barking and growling and then saw tails wagging. "Oh, yes, there you are, K'yon 1 and K'yon 2. My friends. Part of our family, loyal and obedient. Thank you for picking up my scent and saving me. You know I never really could tell you apart." He stopped to pet the two dogs. Oh, so you two want a belly rub. They both rolled over on the lawn. They were chained to a pole but still obedient and loyal, he assumed, to J.J., who had trained them. The real J.J. as he knew her.

So, would this church be used again as a portal? Would there be others who would go on this trip, adventure, "experience"—

whoops—"divine journey?"

Bob knew he would survive the grilling. He was growing and maturing. He could handle these inquiries, which would test his patience and resolve.

As he turned the corner a block away from the church, he felt a wisp of a cool breeze on his cheek. As his face warmed again, he put the word seraphim in his memory bank.

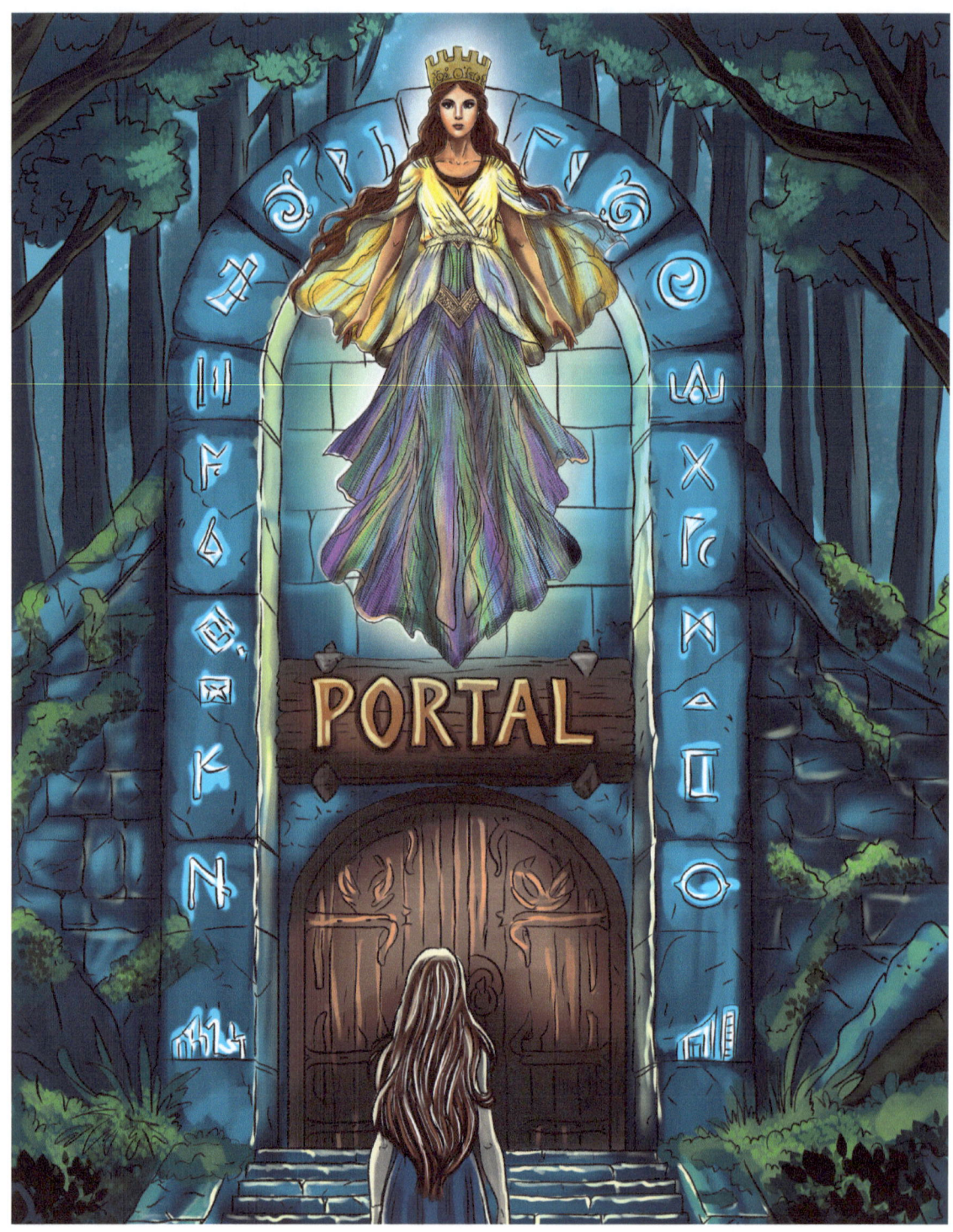

The End

(but really only the beginning)

www.ingramcontent.com/pod-product-compliance
Lightning Source LLC
Chambersburg PA
CBHW041928010726
47507CB00003BA/221